Young Women in Nightclubs

Robert Wexelblatt

ISBN: 978-81-19228-35-5

First Edition: 2023
Rs. 200/-

Cyberwit.net
HIG 45 Kaushambi Kunj, Kalindipuram
Allahabad - 211011 (U.P.) India
http://www.cyberwit.net
Tel: +(91) 9415091004
E-mail: info@cyberwit.net

Printed at Replika.

Acknowledgments

"Young Women in Nightclubs" first appeared in *Belle Ombre*

"TFN" and "Akewi" first appeared in *Scarlet Leaf Review*

"The Adcocks," "Are You A Good Witch or a Bad Witch?" and "I'll Never Know" first appeared in *Blue Lake Review*

"Heautontimoroumenos" first appeared in *Splash of Red*

"Larry's Complete Plumbing Service" first appeared in *Offcourse Literary Journal*

"Beezlepoint and Needleprat" first appeared in *Salt River Review*

"Petite Suite de Renommage" first appeared in *Delmarva Review*

"Franklin W. Dixon" first appeared in *Unlikely Stories*

Cover Illustration, *The Nightclub Singer* by McClelland Barclay, c. 1943

Contents

Young Women in Nightclubs

"They called her the Tenth Muse."

"Muse?"

"Muse. She's a goddess who inspires writers, artists, dancers, poets—you know, that sort of thing. The inspired people were almost all male, of course. I suppose they liked the idea of female assistance."

"But *she* wasn't a goddess, was she?"

"No. And not really a muse, either. Just a girl born on the island Lesbos."

"Lesbos? As in *lesbian*?"

"Uh-huh. Nearly all her poems were lost but the bits we have are mostly about crushes on girls. The most famous and complete is an ode to Aphrodite. I read it for a class."

"Aphrodite?"

"AKA Venus, Goddess of Love. The poem's a prayer begging for her help turning rejection into passion."

"Didn't the men object to poems like that? You know they can't stand feeling left out, that it's against nature and that sort of thing. Reverend Pearson said homosexuality's an abomination."

"Well, they probably did object. I think she was exiled for a while, and maybe that was why. But apparently her poems were *so* good that the men finally overlooked what they were about. Or maybe it didn't bother them so much as it did your Reverend Pearson. The Greeks weren't Methodists, you know; they still aren't. Anyway, Sappho's supposed to have written all kinds of poetry but especially the lyric kind."

"What's that?"

"Poems meant to be sung, accompanied by a lyre, a little harp."

"Were *all* the women on Lesbos lesbians?"

"No. The island had a big city and it turned out a bunch of other writers, all males. But Sappho was the best of the lot. And she loved women. So that's why women who love women came to be called lesbians. Because of her poems. Because she lived on Lesbos."

"Hmm. Well, I kind of like the idea of an island with only women on it like in *Wonder Woman*. Flirting and falling love and praying to goddesses about it and playing little harps. But keeping up the population would be a problem. I mean, no men would mean no babies. Oh, but they could *import* lesbians. In fact, I'll bet lesbians would probably *all* want to immigrate to Lesbos, if it were really an island without men. Imagine. No fathers or brothers, no cigars, no Reverend Pearsons, no pawing, grabbing, stalking."

"Or raping."

"You really think men would stand for it? I mean men like the ones around today?"

"I don't know. I expect a few might find it stimulating, a challenge, maybe exotic. I think women *would* like it, though."

"So, that's where you got your big idea, isn't it?"

"Professor Honigswalt used to say, 'Girls, the classics are always useful.'"

In the decades between V-J Day and the March on Washington, people still went to nightclubs, swanky places that started during the Depression and were located in the lively downtowns of big cities. Suburban couples would make a date for a night out together on the town. Affluent siblings would celebrate their parents' golden anniversary at round tables. Well-off men scored points with first wives or tried to impress prospective second ones. Deals were sealed over the clubs' starched white tablecloths; veterans reunited; proposals of marriage were offered and usually accepted. Young people who could afford it would go to these clubs, take over the dance floor, and wow their elders with their moves. Like everything else in those days, the clubs were rigorously segregated; that is, the patrons were white and the talent often was not. No doubt, the contrast stirred doubts in liberal-minded customers; but, back then, everything about race and gender seemed fixed, all variations pushed into back rooms, under tables, into the alleys of sketchy neighborhoods. And yet, within the crewcut conformist limits of the time, nightclubs still had an air of democracy about them. Gangsters and politicians came, electricians and dentists, welders and district attorneys. All the clubs featured female staff. Young women with heavy cameras and bags of flashbulbs would circulate, taking black-and-white snapshots turned later into glossies and preserved in family albums, everybody dressed to the nines and beaming. Attractive young women, clad less modestly than the photographers, roamed the tables bearing square trays resting against trim midriffs, the Pall Malls, Camels, Chesterfields, Parliaments, and Lucky Strikes all laid out neatly. Still other young women, dressed in demure blazers, took coats and hats by the door, and handed back numbered brass tags. Cocktail waitresses in risqué outfits took orders for alcohol, sex's less sinful cousin. The Brobdingnagian drinks menus featured fancy concoctions like Bullshots, Sidecars, Mudslides, Pink Squirrels, Mai Tais, and Sea Breezes.

It was their good looks that landed these young women their jobs and the tips on which they subsisted. Men with big cigars and flabby jowls sat behind desks and sized them up when they applied. The best looking got to be cocktail waitresses and earned the largest tips. Most of these young women were from out-of-town. They shared studio walk-ups with hotplates and bad plumbing. They talked late into the night about the big tippers and the small, about what sort of men they'd marry, how they deflected the passes made by arrogant head waiters, unctuous sommeliers, entitled bosses, and soused customers. They drowsily rehearsed their high-school adventures and gossiped about movie stars. They picked over the reviews of Broadway shows they hadn't seen and shared the hopeful fantasies that had drawn them to the city. Some, with giggles, fumbling, and various disparagements of men, made experimental love.

Meredith Turner was from the bourgeois stratum of Albany society. Her father was a banker. There were vacations in Florida, trips to Europe, a new Cadillac every other year. She was sent to an expensive private day school after which she enrolled at Vassar. Meredith was a gifted student, bookish, and intended to major in Classics. Midway through her sophomore year, her father's embezzlement was detected. He denied everything right up until he hanged himself the night before the start of his trial. Suddenly, there was no money; the house turned out to be double-mortgaged, and the two life insurance policies had been cashed in years earlier. Meredith's mother went to pieces and was taken in with a bad grace by her brother in Los Angeles. They fixed up the attic for her. Meredith dropped out of Vassar, took the three hundred dollars left in her account, and moved down the Hudson. She found a squalid room in a Bowery fleabag, tore into hunting for a job, and landed one checking coats at The Casbah, a popular nightclub with a phony Levantine décor. Here she met Susie O'Dwyer, a red-headed waitress from Columbia, South Carolina. Susie liked the idea of cutting her rent in half. Meredith moved out of the flophouse and in with Susie who talked incessantly about her ambitions. She already had a stage name and a manager and was going to be a star. However, after her twentieth audition yielded her twentieth rejection and her manager dropped her, Susie had a breakdown. Her Yankee-hating parents came north to retrieve her, to say they'd told her so, and, with smug looks, hauled their defeated daughter back to South Carolina.

Louise Hatterfield grew up in Granville, Ohio. She didn't care for the town, her big Methodist family, or Ohio even if she was homecoming queen, universally admired for her looks. She worked at a drug store through high school and saved her money. It wasn't much but enough for her to take off for New York a week after graduation. She left a brief note for her parents and another for her siblings apologizing for absconding and promising to write. She too applied for work at the Casbah, lied about her age and, once the boss got a look at her, was offered the position of cigarette girl with a promise of promotion to cocktail waitress if things worked out. Louise also found a roommate at the club—Bernice, the club photographer—but Bernice left when she landed a job with a newspaper upstate.

Meredith heard about Louise losing her roommate two days after losing hers and invited her to move in. Louise was grateful. She might have found another roommate and stayed where she was, but she liked Meredith, was impressed by her education and that she was twenty instead of not quite eighteen. She thought of Meredith as a non-Methodist a big sister. Meredith liked Louise too, appreciated her innocence, felt protective, and called her Lou. Their habits and schedules meshed; they wore the same size shoes and tops, and neither dwelt on improbable dreams of fame and fortune. In short, they were compatible. Though they didn't love their jobs, they weren't at all bitter or resentful like some of the girls; in fact, there were things about the work that they valued beyond the tips. They were picking up skills and, for an hour or two each evening, The Casbah felt sophisticated and jolly, even if the gaiety was forced and the high spirits merely alcoholic. Louise learned how to handle men and the women they brought with them. Meredith made a study of how the club worked, spending her breaks interrogating the older staff and people in the kitchen. Practical minded, not consumed with dubious dreams, generally uncomplaining, Meredith and Louise made the best of things.

They persuaded the maître d' to assign them the same night off, Tuesdays. These were for dating patrons who asked nicely, college students Louise met in a diner or, Meredith's case, at a museum or the library. They formed the habit of critiquing the men who asked them out and preferred double dating which facilitated these review sessions and provided an extra measure of protection. Some men sent them jewelry or showed up with flowers and chocolates. These gifts were reviewed as well.

"Roses?"

"Only a half-dozen."

"You like Jim's bracelet?"

"Not really. The thing reminds me of a washed-up welter-weight—too heavy and ugly."

The men fared even worse.

"Tommy has an overbite and that joke about the two secretaries on the escalator? It was just crude. Did you notice that he laughs too loud and spits when he does it?"

"What did I think of Fred? Not a sixteenth as much as *Fred* thinks of Fred."

Late on a Tuesday night that had wound up in a fetid SoHo bowling alley with their dates trying to top each other's score and beer-capacity, Lou and Meredith went to bed together. It was new to them, but they soon figured things out.

"It feels more like remembering than discovering," sighed Louise afterwards.

"Plato," Meredith murmured.

They couldn't wait to get home Wednesday night.

Meredith found a spot in the dingiest part of the East Village; an Italian joint that had gone belly up. She also had a plan for the money they'd need. Everyone they'd invite to join would chip in what they could, but the serious capital would have to come from willing parents, persuadable boyfriends, and sugar daddies. She would only try the banks if she had to.

They knew plenty of talented singers, dancers, and comediennes who'd work for nothing, or almost nothing.

Meredith named the place Sappho's. It would be an all-female nightclub.

"It was really your idea, Lou," she said when she laid it all out.

"Mine?"

"Remember? Your imaginary male-free Lesbos?"

"That?"

"We'll make an island of our own. I think we can recruit all the staff we'll need from The Casbah. The kitchen's already there and fully equipped. The real estate guy swears the plumbing and electricity are up to code. We won't need to spend much on décor; we'll put up posters."

"Of what?"

"Women, of course. The biggest one'll go right by the entrance, a reproduction of Charles Auguste Mengin's portrait of Sappho. You'll love it. She's bare-breasted, brooding, draped in black, leaning on a rock with a lyre hanging from her right hand like a gunslinger's shotgun. Very cool."

"What color's her hair?"

"Jet black."

"Just like yours! So, who else?"

"Culture heroines. Josephine Baker, Isadora Duncan, Mae West, Sarah Bernhardt, Virginia Woolf. I don't know. Maybe Clara Schumann, Djuna Barnes, Martha Graham, a Brontë or two. . . Jane Austen, Mary

Shelley—or her poor mother. There's a poster shop in the Village. We'll see who they've got."

The Casbah had to replace all its young women except for three cocktail waitresses. Two sugar daddies came through; the realtor was eager to get the place occupied and gave them a reasonable rent. They did their own painting, constructed a small stage, had enough money to buy tables, and chairs, cutlery, glassware, and plates from a restaurant remainders store in Chelsea. They stocked the bar with the necessities, recruited a good jazz trio, folk singers, comics. The city was awash with female performers looking for a place to perform. To announce the opening, Meredith had handbills printed and splurged on an ad in the *Village Voice* complete a blurry reproduction of Mengin's *Sappho*. "New Nightclub. Women Only. No Cover."

The place was mobbed from the first night. Young women from downtown came and older ones from uptown, even Westchester County. It was a novelty. Business was brisk and, once they decided to add a cover charge and to price the drinks almost as high as The Casbah, they made enough to give the staff a bit more than minimum wage and to pay back the insistent sugar daddy who hated the club and dropped his mistress. Their other major backer was so infatuated that he didn't ask for anything, just groused good-naturedly about not being able to get in.

Other men were more of a problem. Lou was prescient when she wondered whether the Greeks would have put up with Sappho. There were threatening letters and a brick through the plate glass. An indignant letter to the editor appeared in the *Times*. City inspectors began showing up at a harassing rate.

Women having a good time without them frightened and offended their boyfriends. When one of the waitresses enumerated her beau's complaints, Meredith plucked a wine glass from the bar, held it up, and said, "Behold, the male ego."

One night there was a disturbance or, more precisely, a demonstration. Young men gathered on the sidewalk outside the club. Many were drunk, some angry, and others mocking, but all of them were hostile. Meredith phoned the police who broke it up. Then the police began to show up when there weren't any disturbances. There was an official letter from the City saying steps were being taken to close down the club as a public nuisance. One of the waitresses was dating a public defender who said he'd be glad to take their case, to demand a hearing. He did just that and was so eloquent that he not only got the judge to toss out the case but to ream out the assistant district attorney.

Sappho's was a phenomenon. Some women came because they were sapphic and said it was the only place in the city where they felt comfortable and could be themselves. Others came because they were intrigued or out of feminist solidarity. There were also women who simply wanted a night away from men. The performers began to garner some reviews, to build reputations and snag bookings. Two of them joined the cast of Broadway shows.

Then came the arson. The authorities never found who did it, if they even bothered to look. There were too many suspects. It could have been the miffed boss of The Casbah, any number of disgruntled, threatened boyfriends, felonious defenders of public decency. The proprietor of the failed Italian restaurant had come by after the demonstration ostensibly to express sympathy but also with an offer of "protection," so it could have been the local Mafia whose views on women were presumably in line with the Pope's.

Sappho's went down in flames. The staff scattered. A few left the city returning to wherever they'd come from; some got married, one found a job in retail, two as receptionists, but most as waitresses. Upscale restaurants opened almost daily in the city and all of them were eager to hire attractive female staff. Without knowing it, all the women were waiting around for the Sixties and the Seventies.

"What are we going to do?" Lou asked.

"Move on," said Meredith.

"Together?"

"You have to ask?"

Meredith chose Chicago because it was the country's second biggest city and neither she nor Lou had ever been there. "Virgin territory," she declared cheerfully and with only a little irony.

They found a one-bedroom apartment in a converted Victorian in the Old Town section, the liveliest and most bohemian in the city. It reminded them of Lower Manhattan, except that the buildings weren't as high.

Meredith took a job at the Lincoln Park branch of the Chicago Public Library and Lou was hired as a hostess by the Chicago Cut Steakhouse, a city fixture. Both liked their work and Chicago, even in the winter. They were contented.

For Louise's fortieth birthday, Meredith fished out her old Greek books and made a translation of the opening and closing verses of Sappho's Tithonus poem. She hired a calligrapher to write it out in fancy script on vellum and chose a gilded frame.

Hold fast, little girls, to the Muse's purple gifts

And cling to your sweet lyre, that lover of music.

Eros has given me a beauty not found in the light of day,

The passion and the patience for life that's lost on the young.

They hung the verses beside the one thing that they'd rescued from the fire: Mengin's portrait of Sappho.

TFN

I guess I was no more than five or six when my father sat me down on the first Saturday in May to watch the Kentucky Derby. He was in one of his pedantic moods and determined to explain the whole business to me, from the antebellum lyrics of "My Old Kentucky Home" to why the man with the long bugle wore a red coat to what odds like 7-2 meant. A schoolmaster by profession, it was rare that he went off duty at home. He was big on Learning Experiences, ever on the lookout for Teachable Moments. My mother wasn't like that at all; still, she seemed to find my father's earnest parenting endearing, perhaps because it was so seldom practical, like hers.

The big horses with their tiny, colorful riders were being slowly paraded to the starting gate, almost all escorted by more commonplace, but still pretty, horses ridden by bigger, less tense people, mostly young women in comfortable clothes. Their saddles were larger; *Western* saddles, my father pointed out. He explained that it wasn't the jockeys wanting company but the three-year-old thoroughbreds who needed calming from their *stablemates*, which sounded to me like *playmates*. I knew better than to raise questions, but I didn't see why *both* the jockeys and the horses couldn't use the company. After all, they all must have been jumpy with the big race ahead of them. Even then I thought like that. Typical.

The TV commentators focused on each of the contenders in turn. They spewed information about the horses, their parents and their records, riders, trainers, owners, home stables, how much moisture they liked on a track, and, of course, the odds on whether they'd win. These men knew so much that, for a while, my father gave up and I could just look. One of the three-year-olds had gleaming shanks and long, graceful legs. This animal was so beautiful even the jaded track commentators had to lower their voices and admire; he was that majestic. They referred to the horse as a *chestnut gelding*. My father didn't say anything about what *gelding* meant but did explain that *chestnut* was the horse's color, a rich, deep, glistening brown that was more-than-brown.

This was the memory that came back to me when I walked into Rheinach Hall the first week of my senior year and caught sight of Diane Victoria Mulhorn's hair. It was that same magnificent, riveting chestnut color. I was sufficiently enlightened to be aware of the sin of objectifying a female—worse, only a part of one. Freud might have diagnosed my susceptibility to long hair as an instance of trichophilia or hair fetishism, but I didn't care to analyze my feelings or speculate on their origins. My attraction was simply a personal fact, like my being white, American, and male. I gave no thought to how hard it must be to care for such hair, to wash, dry, and brush it, to carry it around all day knowing people noticed it and some of them might want to touch it, how such a magnificent mane could be a spur to both vanity and self-doubt. I hadn't yet any idea what was under that hair, but love is a close cousin to curiosity: attraction turns into the wish to delve. The nascent scientist admires the butterfly, its flight, its iridescent colors, and is driven to find out how the wings work, even to pull them off. Love and science both want to penetrate. "Even in the desire for knowledge," wrote Nietzsche with a wicked smile under his big mustache, "there is a drop of cruelty."

It's been more than six years since I ignored the opening lecture of the Law and Society course because all my attention was focused on Diane Victoria Mulhorn's hair. Neither of us was taking the class out of interest, but to fulfill a new requirement in something called Social Consciousness. I was getting my degree in Philosophy. My Legal Studies minor was meant to deflect the ridicule attracted by my major. Diane was a double major, and, in my opinion, her two concentrations were ill-matched: History and Public Relations.

Her hair was long, straight, glossy as the thoroughbred's, and I could almost feel it, as if my eyes were fingers. Does it mitigate my crime that I stared with reverence rather than lust? Or that, after falling for her hair, I did the same with the rest of her?

Diane broke off with me three weeks before graduation. What if we'd made it to commencement? Would we then have proceeded hand in hand down a rose-strewn path rather than down our separate, stonier ones? I doubt another three weeks would have made any difference.

After the bust-up, I threw myself into finishing my senior thesis, less out of diligence than grief. During the day, I managed fairly well, but the nights brought welcome/unwelcome dreams. The meaning of some was all too obvious but others were obscure: Diane as a nurse, teacher, go-go dancer; Diane furious, friendly, indifferent, teasing. I can still remember two dreams in which she spoke French, a language she didn't know but I did.

It was thanks to knowing French that I found a summer job as a research assistant. Professor Kardin was writing a book about Samuel Johnson's parliamentary reporting. He explained why this was tricky. Dr. Johnson seldom attended the debates, preferring to invent the speeches while sitting in a coffee house. In those days, there was no official record against which to compare Johnson's version of things. When Professor Kardin and his wife visited Paris that spring, he'd hit on a brilliant idea of how to get an objective account of what was actually said. He figured that the French would have been keenly interested in what the Whigs and Tories were saying to each other. He went to the Quai d'Orsay and, thanks to the influence of a colleague at the Sorbonne, secured a microfilm of letters written by the French hireling who attended parliamentary debates and took notes. With a laugh, he told me that the spy's letters were still marked "Classified"—thus the need for the well-connected colleague and the concealable microfilm. My job was to translate the letters. I found the Frenchman's elegant handwriting as admirable as his inventiveness. Every one of his reports to Paris concluded with a novel way of asking for more money.

The summer felt interminable. I took long bike rides and went home for the July Fourth weekend. In August, my friend Bill invited me to his family's L. L. Bean summer house in Maine for a weekend. It was a matter of killing time, earning a little money before I began post-graduate study, and trying not thinking too much about Diane Mulhorn.

I'd gotten into a good Ph.D. program and, charged with displaced energy, unwilling to pine, I resolved to get my degree in record time and then become an adult. When September came, that's just what I commenced to do. I finished my course work and thesis so rapidly that the faculty seemed more suspicious than impressed. And then I found a publisher. I never expected to hear from Diane Victoria Mulhorn again, certainly not because of a tome on a subject unpopular even with experts in the field.

My monograph is typical of its genre, the revised doctoral thesis aimed at the elusive security of tenure. The editor at the university press that took the manuscript at the urging of my thesis advisor (bless him) insisted I write a new introduction, cut down on the footnotes, replace the *and* in my original title with the standard academic colon. So, the book is titled *Trivalent Logic: The Uses of Subversion*. When Bill said it sounded dry, I told him that the title sounded even more repulsive in German: *Dreiwertige Logik: Die Verwendung von die Untergrabung*. It will be at least a year or probably two before the thing's formally reviewed, if it's reviewed at all. But it has been listed on Amazon. That's how Diane learned of it and broke the radio silence of half-a-dozen years during which the scab formed and hardened, six years in which I secured a doctorate, a job, and a publisher. Also, I married Delia Decairie.

Delia grew up in Atlanta and came north because her father insisted she get a Yankee education. We met at a party thrown by a couple just the obverse of ourselves: Susie was the academic, Dick the business type. Delia had stayed in the north, taking her business degree, and finding a job with Bank of America. That I had a Ph.D. in philosophy made me exotic in her eyes rather than ridiculous; I suppose her MBA did the same for me. Curiosity again, delving, then blooming. After all her years in Yankeeland, Delia doesn't have much of an accent left; however, her diphthongs do tend to lengthen when she gets seductive, angry or, jealous. I'll be keeping Diane's email to myself.

"Hello, Ferguson," Diane's email begins. *Ferguson.* This was her final nickname for me. There had been others, but they were endearments. *Ferguson* was a reference to an old joke I told her about a Yiddish-speaking immigrant who, commanded by an Ellis Island immigration officer to give his name, is terrified and mumbles "*ikh fargesn*" and so got himself renamed Ferguson on the spot. Diane didn't call me Ferguson to remind me of things I'd forgotten but to remind me that I forgot important things.

"Congratulations on the book," she writes. "The bio note on the back says that you're an assistant professor and married, so congratulations on all that, too. I presume the book's your dissertation. At a whopping $176.95 a pop, I don't imagine the press anticipates it's going to sell like hotcakes. And there's no picture on the cover, just words. I bought it anyway, for sentimental reasons. It arrived today and I'm almost up to the introduction. I notice there's no dedication. Is that because you forgot, Ferguson? You really ought to have dedicated it to somebody; I once read that it's bad luck not to. You should have dedicated it to your wife. Or maybe to me. After all, didn't I teach you a little about subversive logic? In my fashion?"

There was a lot more than chestnut hair to admire about Diane Victoria Mulhorn, to wonder at. Here's a handful of adjectives (in alphabetical order): ambitious, complicated, contrary, decisive, elusive, exasperating, exciting, gorgeous, insecure, intelligent, kind, sexy, sweet, tough. As I say, lots to be dazzled by but—no use denying the facts—it started with the fifty minutes I spent staring at the back of her head.

What to do after those fifty minutes? I needed to find out if she had a serious boyfriend. We were seniors; for all I knew, she might be married. But if she were approachable, how was I to go about it? I wasn't any less shy than I'd been in high school and just as undistinguished in the dating department. Beauty simply scared me. That chestnut hair was as intimidating as it was attractive. Both at once. One because of the other.

I conducted some research of the junior-high variety, putting feelers out to my little network. Nobody knew anything about her first year; reports said she'd dated a lot her second year but there'd been nobody serious. In her junior year, there was a boyfriend, but the relationship apparently didn't survive spring break.

You'd think there'd be nothing easier than to strike up a conversation with a classmate. What couldn't you ask about Law and Society? Can you have one without the other? Did you think the lecture on privacy could have used more examples? Why don't we hear more about how society writes its laws or who pays for them? Easy, but still, I couldn't pull the trigger.

About once a week I had dinner with my freshman roommate Mike, a pre-law student masquerading as an English major. Over one of these meals, I babbled about my problem with D. V. Mulhorn. It was embarrassing. He laughed at me and said that I talked about this girl the way philosophers do about their arguments; that is, in a lot more detail than anybody else wants. "Love turns people into bores," he teased. "You, anyway."

"Thanks very much," I grumbled.

"Look," he said, "that hair of hers?"

"Yes?"

"You may think her perfect, superlunary, of virtue all compact and so on; but, in my experience, girls with hair like that care about it quite a lot."

"You think a woman who doesn't care about her hair is—what?"

"A trivial woman? Oh no. Nope. All I'm saying is that she's aware of her hair's effect on guys like you. I'm not saying she's vain or that she grew it that long just to get attention. But what do I know? I certainly don't know her. But then *you* don't either. Who's the trivial one, a woman who prides herself on her hair or a man who's obsessed with it?"

"Obsessed? You think I'm *obsessed*?"

Mike shrugged. "Look, you want to get closer to her, take a risk. Compliment what drew you to her in the first place."

"And how do I do that without looking like a superficial oaf?"

"That presupposes you *aren't* a superficial oaf."

The next night Mike came to my dorm room with a Xerox of W. B. Yeats' poem "For Anne Gregory," the one about how only God could love Anne for anything other than her hair. I didn't know it was famous, but I could see why it deserved to be. Where Yeats had written *yellow*, Mike had crossed it out and penciled in *chestnut*: "And not your ~~yellow~~ chestnut hair."

"Give it to her. And do it with a sheepish grin; you're a natural at sheepish. What've you got to lose apart from self-respect, which you don't have much of anyway? Besides, you'll find out if she's got a romantic streak *and* a sense of humor. And, I'm guessing, if she's, you know. . . interested."

I thought the idea was cheesy, derivative, and high-risk. I put the redacted poem away in a drawer. Eventually, I did give it to her though, once we'd become an item. I enclosed with it a silver and turquoise bracelet I bought her for Christmas. She liked the bracelet, glanced at the poem, smiled indulgently, perhaps ruefully, and said that, if I'd given Yeats to her in September, she'd have sent me packing, pronto.

I had no problem talking with Diane about her history courses but there was some abrasion over public relations. "It's sophistry," I said once and she shot back, "Ever hear of the real-world?" "Reality? PR's all about illusion," I scoffed, and she called me cynical. "Reality, illusion—what's the difference?" I said that PR was about making a bad cause look good. "Maybe, but you get to dress well, and it pays," she pointed out. I tried flattery. "PR's beneath you." "Sweet of you to say, but it's so incredibly easy to get an A," she crowed.

Inevitably, she wearied of defending what she was studying and took to mocking what I was, singling out my favorite class for special ridicule. I'd been mildly interested in the required symbolic logic course I took as a sophomore and so I talked my way into a graduate class on advanced logic and got hooked. At the end of the second week, I persuaded the professor to let me write my senior thesis for him. For me, advanced logic was the intellectual equivalent of chestnut hair. And, like any addiction, it came with consequences.

In our last semester, Diane was kicking back while I was buckling down. She wanted fun and attention; I wanted to work. We fell out of sync. That's the simplest and least disturbing hypothesis about what doomed us—doomed me, anyway.

It was on February 15 that she first called me *Ferguson*. I'd forgotten Valentine's Day.

I tried to defend myself, but I had an ass for a lawyer. "That was very, *very* bad," I admitted. "But I remembered your birthday *and* Christmas. Some credit for that least?"

This argument was met with an icy stare from the bench.

"Hearts all over campus, candy in every shop, flower stalls on the corners. The whole *world's* shouting that it's Valentine's Day and you *still* forgot. Christmas? You don't get any credit for Christmas and, as for my birthday, I reminded you about it *three* times."

I tried to atone by taking her to a new French restaurant, the most expensive place I could think of. But, just a week later, I forgot to ask how her European history midterm had gone. *Ferguson.*

It got worse—I mean, I got worse. I missed our "six-month" anniversary, neglected to text her even once over the long weekend she spent with her friends on the Jersey shore, failed to notice that one of her favorite novelists was reading on campus. A disinterested observer might conclude I was just heaping up straws until I got to the last one.

It was mid-April, and we hadn't seen each other for nearly a week. I'd been working flat out on the thesis but, when I came up for air, I missed her the way a diver misses sky and sun. I was up with the sun on Saturday and put off phoning for as long as I could, which wasn't long at all.

"You woke me up," she declared without either rancor or interest.

"I want to see you. *Need* to."

"That so? Okay. You can buy me a gigantic latte at Renzo's in like half an hour and then I'll tell you a story."

She'd put on jeans and an old, stained sweatshirt. Her hair needed washing; it was flat and stringy. I'd never seen it like that before and, with a jolt, realized this was because she didn't care. A bad sign. She rubbed her eyes and took a big gulp of latte.

The story was about her parents. She hadn't told me much about them and I hadn't asked. Logic notwithstanding, I was one of those romantics who imagine that the objects of their affection floated in from the sea on a half-shell, born the moment they're first seen. If I thought about Mulhorn *mère et père* at all, it was as abstract parents: standard-issue, middle-class, essential yet insignificant.

The story began without any preamble.

"My mother was dentist. She practiced for years and years and made a good income, more than my father. He'd trained as a social worker and burnt out fast. As a teenager his hobby was collecting coins. He subscribed to numismatic magazines and enjoyed looking through them the way other boys did *Playboy*, I suppose. He did a little trading, nothing much. At some point Dad decided that he liked silver dollars more than his desperate clients—the poverty, messed-up kids, the drugs, despair, and crime. So, he quit his job and set up as a coin dealer. Mom ran the house, did the disciplining, cooked, shopped, cleaned, went on fixing teeth. Dad was much happier and busy in a good way, always on the phone or the computer, going off to coin dealer conventions. It was funny in a way. He was immersed in money but didn't make much. I suppose the old coins were like works of art to him. He left more and more stuff for my mother to do—the bills, the insurance, their social calendar, dripping faucets, peeling paint. 'You take care of it,' he'd say blithely. And Mom *did* take care of it. All of it. At dinner he'd talk about his day with enthusiasm and never ask about hers. Looking at coins was interesting; looking into mouths was disgusting. At some point—maybe after he'd forgotten their anniversary—she stopped telling him much of anything.

"One afternoon while Mom was fixing dinner and I was doing my algebra homework, Dad opened the local newspaper and read that real estate taxes would be going up five percent. According to the article, this was because the town manager had proposed the increase at a council meeting and argued for it so forcefully—the starving schools, the potholed streets—that they gave in, almost unanimously. 'Who's this town manager?' he demanded. And that's how he found out."

I guessed where this was going. I could tell Diane wasn't about to point out the moral for me.

"Your mother was the town manager?"

"Bingo."

"She'd quit being a dentist and didn't mention it to him?"

"Yep."

"Come on. Really? You're exaggerating."

She leaned back—that is, away from me.

"Freud had this theory," she said.

"I thought you despised Freud."

"I do. I mean, *penis* envy? Right. But that doesn't mean I think he's necessarily wrong. About everything, I mean."

"So you pick the parts you like?"

"Of course I do. I pick the parts where he's right."

I thought this over and speculated, hesitatingly. "So, you think you like me because I remind you of your father, but now you're raking me over the coals for being like him?"

She sipped her latte. "Maybe."

I threw up my hands.

"I'm a person, a woman," she said, "not a logician. Don't go looking for consistency in all the wrong places."

I thought the story about her parents was improbable, invented or at least dolled up, but knew better than to say so. I took another tack. "You're proud of your mother, aren't you?"

"Of course."

"Prouder of her than your father?"

"I'm proud of my father too. For other things."

"Other than what kind of husband he is?"

"I told you. Mom did discipline. What Dad did was unconditional love. He had the time for it. He's a perfect father, up to a point. But everybody's everything only up to a point."

I foolishly tried a weak joke. "Did *he* remember your birthday?"

She replied sharply. "He *always* does. And without any reminders."

I thought I got the point. Diane Victoria Mulhorn would not be marrying an inattentive man, one like her father, or me. Even unconditional love wasn't enough.

"And so? I'm not forgiven, am I?"

She sighed, exasperated, or resigned. "If there's such a thing as a confirmed female bachelor then I'm pretty sure that's what I'm going to be."

Exasperated and resigned. Despising and adoring her father. Admiring her mother and rebelling against her. Vain about her hair and indifferent to her appearance. Fascinated by the historian's inquiry into the truth, drawn to the public relations expert's dexterity in falsifying it. Attracting, repelling. A person, not a logician.

And which was I? Both? Neither? Something else?

Trivalent, or Three-Value, Logic undermines classical logic by adding to its two values (true or false) a third (neither). T, F, and N. Diane Victoria Mulhorn isn't wrong; she really did teach me something about it. She taught me that N can mean any number of things.

N can mean "I haven't got a clue."

N can mean "Perhaps."

N might mean "not defined."

N could even mean "nonsense. . . arrant poopwhistle!"

N can mean "both true *and* false, a little of each."

N can mean “one or the other” (“Amanda isn’t nice but she’s not nasty either”).

N can mean “not knowable” (“What was there before the Big Bang? If there’s an all-powerful, all-loving God, why were these babies slaughtered?”)

Introducing N into classical logic disrupts its purity, saturates it with uncertainty, sows contradiction, paradox, and confusion. Introducing N into classical logic renders it unserviceable by drawing it nearer to the way things are. Nobody likes it. Even the cybernetic geniuses haven’t found a use for it.

Diane’s email concludes this way:

“You’ll be horrified to learn that I’m not only working in public relations but have turned out to be rather good at it. In fact, I’ve just opened my own outfit. Good client list, four employees, all nice, smart kids. No philosophy majors. I do a lot of *pro bono* work to make up for the *pro nobis* kind. I’ll assume you haven’t Googled me, even though I’ve Googled you. So, click on the link below to see what my hair looks like these days and the stuff under it.

“PS - My mother retired to take care of my father full time. Dad’s forgotten almost everything.

“As for me, I remain a confirmed female bachelor. Am I happy? Happy in my unhappiness, never lonely in my solitude? TFN. How’s that for an answer, Professor?”

The Adcocks

Nobody foresaw what took place at last year's town meeting. The agenda was as dull as ever. There were no pothole or snow-removal crises. The water was colorless and flowed on demand. The sewers weren't backed up, and the high school was sending its graduates on to the customary colleges and universities. The town budget was substantially unchanged from the year before; and, as nobody was proposing a property tax increase, attendance was no greater than usual.

Yet there was a scene, an explosion. Intemperate things were said, regrettable words spoken, and the consequence was that the Adcocks moved away.

We supposed it wouldn't take long for the memory to fade. Many of us would have liked to forget about the Adcocks and the town meeting. People move all the time, we said; they relocate, retire, divorce, die. Nothing out of the ordinary has happened. We certainly didn't expect to miss the Adcocks, and it's not as if we dwell on them—on the contrary. We speak about them seldom and usually in whispers. But the whispering signifies that we do remember, that some of us are ashamed and we miss Roland, Lena, Bertrand, and Joanie.

The Adcocks were a standard-issue suburban family in nearly every respect. They lived in one of the colonials on Hancock Street, owned a late-model Honda CRV and an old Toyota Corolla. The kids were polite, good in school, athletic, and had plenty of friends. Roland was district manager with a data firm. Lena was generous in both her nature and proportions, an earth-mother everybody loved. For the most part, the Adcocks were ordinary members of the community, liked and respected. Yet there were problems, though *problems* doesn't feel like a satisfactory word. Maybe *snags* or *hitches*. Except for Lena, each of the Adcocks had something that stuck out where it should have been smooth, some small bump that abraded.

The August after they moved to town, some ten years back, the Adcocks were invited to a neighborhood barbecue by the O'Connors.

Roland was stout but not flabby, a little under average height, with a round face that exuded good nature. He wore his brown hair closely cropped which made his ears stick out. He had a habit of stroking his chin especially when he was going to speak at length, as if he were checking on his shave or missed having a beard.

At some point that evening, after a few beers, Fred O'Connor asked Roland about his name.

"So, Roland. That's an unusual name."

Roland Adcock smiled and rubbed his chin then explained in a way Fred later described rather confusingly as serious and at the same time not.

"My mother was from Mobile, Alabama and romantic in the way of southern belles. In her case, the fascination was with knights—not nighttime, *medieval* knights, with a k. Did you know that before the Civil War the bestselling books in the South were all by Sir Walter Scott? *Ivanhoe* was my mother's favorite. The War stuck a pin in that inflated, flowery stuff for lots of Southerners, but not all. A harmless thing, really, but she called me Roland after the Frankish hero—Hruolandus in Frankish, Orlando in Italian, Roland in French. When my son was born, to please my mother, I called him Bertrand, after Bertrand du Gueslin, another famous French knight."

"How about your little girl?"

"Joanie? After Jeanne d'Arc. She was a knight, too, you know."

"No kidding?"

"Sure. Then there's the dog."

"Your dog?"

"When the kids picked him out at the pound, I called him Otto. Otto von Estenfeld was a famous Teutonic knight. The mutt just didn't look French."

Then Frank and Roland had a laugh and another beer. The name business was unusual, but that wasn't Roland's eccentricity, not the one that rubbed people the wrong way. That came out for the first time—but not the last—at the next year's July Fourth picnic.

Roland got into this discussion with Bill and Jill Meyer and Harold Baer. Apparently, it began when Harold said something about patriotism and the Revolutionary War. Roland rubbed his chin.

"The colonists were brave but also greedy."

"What do you mean greedy?" Jill asked.

"They should have paid up for British military protection."

"Who from?"

"The French, but mostly the Indians."

"Native-Americans," Jill corrected.

Roland went on. "Slavery would have ended far earlier under British rule. In fact, the southern colonies rose up when the British promised their slaves freedom. Greed again. And racism, of course. The Brits outlawed the slave trade in 1807 and enforced it. There would have been no Civil War. The colonists won because of French aid which helped to bankrupt France and brought on their revolution and so the reign of Terror and the Napoleonic Wars. The love of liberty, everybody being equal, consent of the governed—who couldn't applaud these ideals. But the war? Sheer hypocrisy—a war of liberation led by slave owners. And the colonists' guerrilla tactics made war even less civilized than it had been up till then."

"But that's how we won," said Bill, an Air Force veteran.

"You'd prefer that we stayed British?" Jill asked, genuinely astonished.

"Look at Canada today," said Roland. "Free and sovereign as the US but also more humane and less disorderly. And on the metric system, too."

At this point Bill got heated. "Why don't you move to Canada then, you like it so much, *eh*?"

"Some of my forebears did just that. But I'm not Canadian and I'm not British. I'm as American as you are, Bill."

"*Are* you?" said Harold. "If you don't think much of the Declaration or the Revolution, I'd say that's in question."

"Harold, calm down," whispered Jill.

"It's not a requirement of citizenship to support anything," said Roland with a smile.

"Thanks to the Revolution!" Harold retorted.

"Well, not really. Thanks to centuries of European political philosophy and the framers of the Constitution, who read it."

Later, everybody who was there agreed that Roland sounded pompous but also that he remained entirely calm. He just rubbed at his chin and smiled at them indulgently, exasperatingly sure of himself.

Roland Adcock may have looked the same as always—stout, with that open, round, good-natured face—but, after the story went the rounds, people didn't look at Roland in quite the same way.

Bertrand Adcock didn't start for the high-school football team, but he played in every game. He had his father's physique, so he was made a guard. Bertrand was an officer of the Service Club and not just to please his philanthropic mother. He organized a successful food drive on his own. His grades were solid and he never got into trouble. There was just the one thing: after he got his license, he drove the old Corolla into Detroit every Saturday to study with the imam of a mosque. His best friend, Ronnie Freeland, mentioned this to his mother Betty, who was troubled. When she ran into Lena Adcock at the dry cleaners, she got up the nerve to ask about it.

"You aren't at all worried?"

"Well," said Lena, "I was raised a Quaker and Roland was raised an Episcopalian. We sent the kids to Sunday School at Saint Emmanuel's. Joanie still goes, but Bertrand decided to stop when he was eleven. Now he's curious, and we think that's just fine. Don't you?"

Neither Betty Freeland nor the women she told thought it was fine.

Bertrand was a popular boy and solidly built. Nobody went after him at school; there was no bullying, hardly any teasing. The boy seemed the same as ever. He didn't go around quoting the Qu'ran, dressing up in white robes, or look like he was trying to grow a beard. He didn't talk about his visits to the mosque but, when asked, he didn't deny them either.

Warren Olson, one of his teammates, asked him about going into Detroit.

"Aren't you scared?"

Bertrand grinned and said he'd never run into any trouble there and had made a bunch of new friends.

"I mean, but why, you know, *Islam*?"

Bertrand, smiling all the while, explained that he thought life in America—or at least our town—might have become just a bit too easy and maybe a little empty.

"People talk about the stuff they own and want to be entertained all the time, binge-watching and shopping online, sexting and vaping and drinking. Nothing's sacred and hardly anything isn't allowed. You know? I mean, there's nothing wrong about the stuff we do. It's not that. But people think about themselves too much and they wonder whether anything means anything and maybe it doesn't, but at the mosque they look at things differently."

"Are you going to *convert* or something?"

Bertrand shrugged. "I'd have to be something to convert *from*. I guess I'm like a poor guy in a jewelry store. Just looking."

His friends may have been okay with Bertrand's going to Detroit, but the word for how we grownups looked at Bertrand would be *askance*.

Lena, the earth-mother, wasn't concerned about her husband's being a Tory or her son learning to be a terrorist. In fact, she didn't appear to care. If anybody criticized them, she didn't exactly fight back, didn't defend them or their views individually. She just said cheerfully that everybody had a right to think whatever they wanted. We took this to mean she was just as accepting of our criticism as of her family. It was disarming. Lena was sweetness itself. She never got angry. She loved everybody.

Yet Lena attracted a kind of criticism, too. Some women, including my wife, thought she could be a lot more attractive if she'd put a little effort into it, that she was too crunchy and dressed like a hippie and could stand to lose some weight. "Vegetarians eat too much cheese," declared my wife, the dietary expert. But there wasn't any malice in all this. On the contrary, the idea was that if Lena could just dress a bit more fashionably, use a little makeup, and drop ten pounds, then she'd be happier. Everybody could see she was content; but, to some of her neighbors, this contentment seemed like settling, like resignation. Though they weren't exactly contented themselves, they thought that if she were more like them, she'd be happier.

Lena didn't just love everybody; she also wanted to feed everyone. Soon after they moved to Hancock Street, Lena had the two big arbor vitae in the backyard taken down and rototilled the whole thing. She planted some flowers and a few spireas, but mostly vegetables and herbs. The yard was really a small farm, and Lena worked in it almost every morning. When the crops came in, there was always an over-abundance. She supplied her neighbors with tomatoes, zucchini, summer squash, pole and string beans, strawberries, lettuces, carrots, potatoes, parsnips, and herbs. The leftovers she put out on a table by the curb with a brightly painted board that said FREE!

She also did volunteer work, visiting the elderly, reading to toddlers at the library, was on call two nights a week for the local Samaritans. Then her son's food drive gave her an idea.

She drove the Corolla to the exurbs and beyond to visit local farmers. She must have charmed them. The result was our popular Thursday farmers' market. She made sure there were always a couple of crates of produce set aside for Bertrand to take with him to Detroit on Saturdays.

If anyone tried to thank her for setting it all up, Lena wriggled with pleasure and embarrassment inside her mumu.

"Oh no," she'd say, "thank *you* for coming. It makes me so happy."

Joanie Adcock was a little blonde thing, the slightest bit plump. She was smart, maybe even precocious. Her face was as sweet as her mother's and open as her father's. Her voice was high-pitched but firm and winning. She was charming even after she turned serious. This seriousness began during her last year of middle school when she started to listen to NPR. The one thing she wanted for Christmas was her own subscription to the *Detroit Free Press*. Apart from that, Joan Adcock was by all accounts an ordinary enough thirteen-year-old girl just becoming interested in boys, anxious about her looks and clothes, playing soccer, listening to music, texting back and forth with friends.

All the ninth-graders had to do a final project for Social Studies. It was a state requirement not taken very seriously by most of the students, not in June with school almost over, nor, for the same reason, by their teachers. It was box-checking. Go online, cut and paste a report (with citations) on something like the transcontinental railroad or the Battle of Bunker Hill, Henry Ford, Edwin Muir, the Erie Canal, the history of online gaming. Anything would do.

Probably because of NPR, the *Free Press*, and her big brother's stories about Detroit, Joanie decided to do a report on how the Brown v. Board of Education decision affected school integration in the area. She read the 1954 decision and several articles about it. She researched white flight and the deterioration of the Detroit schools that followed. This led her to the case of Milliken v. Bradley. By then, she had evidently become, if not obsessed, then passionate and indignant.

Here's a short version of Joan's report: In 1970, the NAACP sued the state of Michigan over school segregation in Detroit. The distinctive point in the suit was that it demanded the inclusion of the suburbs in a desegregation plan. The NAACP pointed out that the city's population was by then largely black and that of the suburbs white. Therefore, any desegregation plan limited to the Detroit school district would be completely meaningless.

A federal district judge named Stephen Roth heard lengthy testimony on why and how Detroit was black and the suburbs white. He agreed with the NAACP that residential segregation in the metropolitan area was the result of government policy going so far as to say that, if the boundaries of Detroit's school district had been drawn up in 1970, they'd have been unconstitutional. Judge Roth's order was not to alter those boundaries, though, but to have white suburban kids enroll in Detroit schools and vice versa. The decision was immediately appealed.

The Supreme Court overturned Judge Roth by a 5-4 vote in 1974, exactly two decades after the Brown decision—a coincidence made much of by Joanie. The Supreme Court's majority held that the government had nothing to do with residential segregation in Detroit and so no remedy was called for. Joanie, who had done her research assiduously, wrote that, only days before the decision was issued, the mayor of Dearborn told the *New York Times*, "I favor segregation." He also remarked on the record, "Every time we hear of a Negro moving. . . in, we respond quicker than you do to a fire."

Perhaps a few of our oldest residents had some vague memory of this history, but most of us learned of it when they heard about Joanie Adcock's report.

How you see the upshot of Milliken v. Bradley depends, of course, on your point of view. To white suburbanites, like us, people who'd fled Detroit and taken on scary mortgages and high taxes to send their children to better schools, the decision was both fair and wise, sparing us the disorder of court-ordained interference and ensuring the fruits of our sacrifices. The other view was that the Court had at a stroke exempted the entire North from the desegregation it imposed on the South. In his thundering dissent, Thurgood Marshall called it "a giant step backwards."

Joanie Adcock saw things the same way.

Our annual town meeting was scheduled, as always, for the second week in June, just before the school year ended and people began to scatter to summer vacations. On the first of the month, Joan Adcock took herself to Town Hall and the Office of the Council. She handed Justine Bullock, our Council secretary, a flawlessly typed request to be included on the meeting's agenda.

Justine read it, smiled at the girl.

"I think it's just wonderful that you're so civic-minded."

It was a patronizing response, and our popular Council President, George Whitmarsh, reacted the same way.

"Well, *this* is a first," he said jovially to Justine when she handed him Joanie's petition. "I don't see why we can't give the kid a few minutes at the end. It's good to encourage young people."

Neither Justine nor George thought to ask Joanie why she wanted to speak or about what.

The auditorium in our century-old Town Hall might once have held the entire citizenry. Now it's too small for a mass meeting but serves for recitals by visiting B-list musicians, awards ceremonies, hearings of no general interest, and the annual town meeting. It's a handsome room, with walnut wainscoting on two sides, high windows, an iron chandelier, and a low stage upfront. There are two fading WPA murals on opposing walls. The one on the left romantically depicts a hygienic Ottawa or Chippewa village with good-looking women in fringed buckskin skirts and cherubic children playing outside two tidy lodges. Four muscular braves are just emerging from the surrounding forest with a dead, but bloodless buck, a twelve-pointer. On the right, in the same style and probably by the same artist, is a rendering of the town as it might have looked decades before it got paved roads, fast-food franchises, post-war subdivisions and McMansions—an idealized farming town, clean and innocent, with hitching posts, a dry goods store, and a blacksmith shop.

When the dull business of the town meeting was finished, George Whitmarsh turned his best smile on the small crowd.

"Now, everybody, we've something out of the ordinary to wind up this year. One of our town's public-spirited students has asked to address the meeting for a few minutes. So, please don't anybody get up and leave. Miss Adcock?"

Clutching her report to her chest, Joan got up from her seat in the front row, took the two steps on to the stage and went to the podium. George, still smiling, lowered the microphone for her and made a kind of gallant flourish with his arm. "The floor's all yours, my dear."

Without any preliminary remarks, Joan read her report. It took fifteen minutes. It was bit like a lecture delivered by a humorless little professor with a charming soprano voice.

When she ended the reading, George, minus the smile now, got up to thank her and adjourn the proceedings. Joanie stopped him.

"Please. I'm not finished."

"You're not? I beg your pardon," George growled.

Joan Adcock laid aside her report and looked out over the hall.

"I couldn't find anything in the Milliken decision that forbids *voluntary* integration. In fact, there have been some successful programs doing that in Boston and Milwaukee. These programs are successful but they're tiny. Only a handful of city kids get bussed to suburban schools. I think Judge Roth had the right idea. So, I'm formally proposing a resolution that we set up an *exchange* program with the Detroit Public School District. I also propose that we pool our school funding with Detroit's until the same is spent on everybody and every child can get a decent education no matter where they happened to be born."

Bertrand, sitting by himself way in the back, leapt up.

"I second the proposal!"

The crowd pretty much erupted and George, frowning now, moved himself between Joan and the microphone.

"Both the proposal and the second are out of order. Neither this child nor the person seconding her proposal is a registered voter."

"I am!" shouted Roland Adcock over the din of the crowd. He stood up beside his wife who went on knitting contentedly. "I'm a registered Republican!"

That's when it began to turn ugly, with booing, catcalls, scornful laughter.

"Ridiculous!"

"Absurd!"

"Damned socialist nonsense!"

"Who's this kid to preach at us?"

"Yeah, who does she think she is? Self-righteous brat!"

"This town isn't racist—"

"If anybody thinks I'm going to—"

"Never—"

Then it got worse.

"These Adcocks," somebody said loudly. "Roland hates America."

"And the boy's a jihadist."

"That little girl's been brainwashed."

"Liberalism gone nuts."

At this point, Lena put down her knitting, labored to her feet, and walked slowly to the front of the hall.

"It's Lena."

"Oh."

The noise quieted some.

Lena made her way on to the stage and to the podium, excusing herself as she elbowed George out of the way. She raised the microphone and looked over the room with a wan and melancholy but affectionate smile.

"It's really too bad," she said. "I love this place and all of you, my neighbors, and I love the farmers we're lucky to have all around us. We've become close, I like to think. But, after hearing what you think of my family—and especially my brave, smart, and decent Joanie—I'm afraid the time's come for us to move."

And with that, Lena lumbered down from the stage like a woman with bad knees and made her way up the center of the suddenly silent auditorium, with its Depression-era murals of the Indian lodges and dead buck, the dry goods store and the blacksmith shop. Her family followed and, before the month was out, so were the Adcocks.

Heautontimoroumenos

When I came in from my run at about ten-thirty Dushka was hunched under the dining-room table wearing a black bra and pink panties. She didn't take the trouble to come out and look at me but at least she mumbled "Uh-um?" This might possibly have meant "Good run?" I'd have preferred her to scrutinize my complexion, maybe observe that it was too purple, worry about my blood pressure. "Uh-um?" could just signify indifference.

When I had slipped out of the bedroom an hour earlier Dushka's sleeping breath rose musical and sweet, her face somber as a warden's. Dushka is an earnest sleeper.

In my shorts and soaking T-shirt, I stood by the table in the teak and chromium dining room of my ostentatiously capacious condo. I've got the whole fifth floor and the elevator opens right onto my living room.

I asked Dushka what she was doing down there.

"Writing a letter," she said.

"Under the table?"

Her answer was slow in coming, which was ominous. "On that part of the floor over which looms the table. Yes." Dushka doesn't care for rhetorical questions. But then, who does?

I made for the bathroom, yanking my T-shirt over my head as I went.

Maybe Dushka thought she should force herself to pay attention to me because she quietly observed, "You ought to try it."

"Try what?"

Her voice came from leagues away. "Children love caves and forts. Wombs. Restrictions can be inspirational. It's well known. You ought to try some. Really."

I didn't stop. I called over my shoulder. "I'm taking a shower. Want one?"

"With *you*? Sex maniac."

My suggestion had nothing to do with sex and she knew it. I was hinting that Dushka could maybe use a shower. I know how to get a rise out of her when I need to. I've learned a few things about women, at least about Dushka. The slightest criticism about her personal hygiene will do the trick, though it's a risky tactic.

"I showered when I got up. You're not inferring—"

Her volume had gone up. I matched it. "The word's *implying*, and I wasn't."

Now that we were shouting, she didn't seem so far away, which was the whole point.

As I turned the shower on, she was still protesting. "You don't grasp the nature of depression. I've done my—"

I got right under the spray, let it pound my scalp. When you've worked up a virtuous sweat hot water smells good. While soaping, I fretted again about this putative depression of Dushka's. Dr. Fein, the psychiatrist I sent her to, despite the potentially terrific financial incentive for saying yes to the diagnosis, said no. No, not clinically depressed, said Fein. Drugs? No again, medication was not indicated. He didn't hold with all these happy pills, he said, then leaned back in his black leather chair, a man as bloated with wisdom as a fat tick with blood. He looked at me skeptically and tendered his conclusion with admirable concision. "Dushka's only intermittently sad." That was the whole of his diagnosis to me, the bill-payer. *Intermittently sad*. I nodded at the doctor, a man-to-man nod. I believed him simply because he had called her *Dushka* and not *your friend* or *the young lady*. I thanked him and even felt grateful for the phrase. *Intermittently sad* did hit the nail on the head, I guess. Having filled me in, Fein summoned Dushka from the waiting room and repeated his two-word diagnosis. The young lady took it calmly. She agreed that sadness was what she felt and that her melancholy came and went. She posed no questions, apparently accepting the justice of Fein's verdict just as I did. "Isn't it the same for you?" she asked me in bed that night. "Or are you different from other people, immune to the human condition? I've heard money can do that."

"Me? Oh, I'm completely average. Size medium everything. *You're* the odd one. And you shouldn't overestimate what money does. People always do."

I turned over and regretted referring to Dushka as both odd and commonplace, as "people." She lay beside me, perfectly still and quiet, though in her head she might have been playing Paganini.

I got out of the shower. Dushka was still scribbling away, crouched under the table, intent as a diamond cutter.

I donned my robe and, toweled my hair, padded back into the dining room. "Who's the letter to?"

"Minister of the Interior."

"Thug of the month?"

"It's not easy but I thought I'd write him a poem. Poetry profits from enclosed spaces. Some of it, anyway. Sonnets, for instance. Haiku."

"And limericks?"

I had an impulse to tease. This goes way back with me, long before Dushka. Teasing is the tactic my shyness adopted to cope with feminine creatures—also small children and immature men.

"Now, Dushka, if it's so difficult to write the Interior Minister a poem, why don't you just copy the letter Amnesty supplies? Isn't that what everybody else does? I mean you take it down to the corner, ask them to copy it, you sign it, do an envelope—"

She teased back in her elegant fashion. "Your notion of humor would stagger anybody not inured to it," she said. Then she went on more earnestly. "Think of how easy it must be to ignore a couple thousand Xeroxed letters that all say the same thing, especially if you're a sadistic bastard in a big office who doesn't even open his own mail. Repetition turns meaning to mush. Fuck fuck fuck fuck fuck fuck. See?"

"Love love love love," I said, no longer teasing as I loped into the bedroom to get dressed. I felt hurt but didn't care to show it, though I'm not above luxuriating in a display of bruised sensitivities. In fact, I have a talent for complaining. The secret is that whenever I pretend to be more hurt than I am I instantly become as hurt as I pretend to be.

I began to dress. "Anyone call?"

She didn't answer.

"*Anybody call*?"

"What? For *you*?"

"For *any*body."

"Well, nobody called *me*. It was just me and the Interior Minister. Hey, maybe I should call *him*. A long-distance telephone call—that would be impressive, wouldn't it? That might get his attention. And, if I could manage to sound just the least bit sexy, maybe I could get this poor history teacher out of the dungeon they're torturing him in."

I came back into the dining room. "So, you don't think your poem's so hot?"

"Maybe the Interior Minister doesn't care for poetry. Maybe he won't get it. It might make him angry. Interference in internal affairs."

As she was still under the table, I couldn't see Dushka's face, only her small feet, a tender bit of ankle. I once told her that she had unusually good-looking feet and for months she went barefoot inside the apartment. In the winter, her feet turned blue, and I had to amend my compliment. I told her I didn't find her feet attractive; I said it was more a matter of their not being repellent, which is what most female feet are, for me at least. Thereupon Dushka kept me up half the night interrogating me about my attitude toward feminine pedal appendages. "How many women have asked you to rub their feet? Do women's feet smell bad to you? When you see women at the beach do you avoid looking at their feet? At about what age do you think a girl's feet become bad looking? Do large feet on women especially offend you? You remember Baudelaire: *Tes pieds sont aussi fins que tes mains.* Pushkin had a thing for women's feet too. Does this make you think less well of their poetry?" Dushka does this fairly often. The more probing her rata-tat-tat questioning, the less coherent my replies. It can be stupefying. I never refuse to respond but my answers become vaguer, more nebulous. In the end, I just turn submissive, saying anything, agreeing to everything. At three a.m. I told her that I had lied, that both her feet were precious to me, that Baudelaire and Pushkin had nothing on me in that department. I even took one of them in hand and gave the sole a rub. . . anything to get the light out. "What a bear you are. I knew it all along," Dushka purred.

"As it happens my poem's terrific. All my poems are, at first; it's only later that they turn bad. Like my mother's casseroles. Would you like to listen to it? I'm already on the third draft."

"Fire away," I said tightening the belt on a pair of chinos.

The first time I saw Dushka she was still a child prodigy, playing the chilly Sibelius *Violin Concerto*. At the time I hadn't much interest in music and none at all in Sibelius, whose name sounded like a Roman Emperor's. Concerts not only bored but disgusted me. I am a child of the electronic age and the sight of rather ordinary-looking people sawing, puffing, and pounding away embarrassed me. Because I was single and not poor, the ferociously cultured wife of a business associate hectored me into becoming a patron of the Orchestra. She accomplished this with the energy other women of her age and inclinations expend on matchmaking: a single man in possession of a good fortune and all that. Among the *nouveau riche* in those days, I was *le plus nouveau* and this gentle lady, whose family had been rich for two generations, whose grandfather's pushcart had long ago found its place among the family legends, eagerly enfolded me with her muscular wing and shoved me into Society. Society seemed to me a Cartesian grid whose x and y axes were quantity of assets and the number of years they had aged. Her advice to me came in fiats. I saw her not as a member of an intimidating elite, but as a woman of a certain age to whom obedience was owed simply because she expected it. In no time I found myself on several boards and my name began breaking out on brass plaques like acne on an adolescent. Her intent was to make of me a notorious philanthropist, and philanthropy consisted chiefly in my presenting large checks to her favorite institutions.

The night I first clapped eyes on Dushka she was only just fifteen but already a veteran. She wore a bow in her hair like those favored by schoolgirls in old Soviet newsreels. Because puberty had not visibly descended on her, Dushka looked about eleven, a doll in a party dress. Because of this childishness the serious look she threw the conductor to indicate that she was ready for action struck me as comical, completely at odds with everything I believed about the levity of prepubescent girls. This was, by the way, the same determined look that spreads over Dushka's countenance in sleep, thus a truth of her nature. Dushka's seriousness runs silent and deep. I was twenty-three at the time and, despite what could justly be called a dearth of experience with girls either pubescent or pre, I figured I knew what they were like. I could understand this child being terrified—overdressed people, imperious maestro, envious gaggle of grown-up first and second violinists hoping the brat would screw up—but surely no one so young could be that *grave*. Even her name wasn't serious enough. *Dushka* sounds like an Eastern European endearment; Papa fixes his gaze on the apple of his eye, opens wide his peasant's arms, and croons "Ah, come to me, you little dushka." That intent grimace did not change as she played a theme I'd never heard before, but which instantly filled me with unfocused nostalgia. It wasn't Sibelius' lyricism, but Dushka's look that bowled me over. I couldn't get over it: all that discipline and intelligence seemed too adult for such a little girl.

As Dushka recited her poem from under the table she knocked her feet together, one arch nestling briefly into the other, beating out an irregular rhythm, as she modulated her voice from earnest and angry to wistful and lofty. There were pairs of Dushkas. Monkey/nightingale. Crusader/poet. Prodigy/woman. And all of them were serious.

"*Your Excellency: I would like to draw to your attention the case of Milovan Mastarovic, a thirty-six-year-old teacher of history. Should Your Excellency meet a zaftig woman in a civet-scented pied à terre would your boots impress her carpet as they do the pliant shag of history? Mastarovic was sentenced by the district court of Doboj to three years two months for (pardon my liberty in quoting) 'maliciously and untruthfully portraying socio-political conditions' in your country. May you always, Excellency, portray each subject, your outstanding self included, truthfully and may your unmalicious socio-political renditions gratify the most orthodox tomcats of downtown Doboj. Excellency, may I beg you to cast your all-seeing eye upon Article Nineteen of the International Covenant on Civil and Political Rights which, perhaps in a giddy access of post-War enthusiasm, your nation signed and the which you blithely ignore as you bound down brown Doboj boulevards ogling rear-ends, your thick face turned toward the irreproachable national socio-political conditions while history, like an ignorable breeze, blows backwards all untaught for three whole years, two whole months.*"

I knelt by the table, sighed, and kissed her ankle.

I decided to take Dushka out for dinner. As she dressed, I watched the news, which, notwithstanding the well-fed *joie de vivre* of the anchorman and anchorwoman, was anything but good. She came out of the bedroom sporting a long maroon dress I hadn't seen before. Over it lay the familiar, much loved fringed black lace shawl left her by her great aunt Bronja. She spun around expertly, perhaps in emulation of her friend Germaine, that feline genius of the catwalk.

"How do I look?"

"Like a Victorian lampshade."

Dushka broke into her wickedest woman in Chelsea accent, something that she also picked up from Germaine. "I say! Victorian lampshade—exactly the look I was after, old chap!"

It was a pleasantly warm evening and we strolled over to Simonelli's. On the way, Dushka asked me for ten dollars to give to a disreputable, bulky man leaning in a doorway. She assumed he was homeless and hungry though possibly he was just loitering and overweight. He had the look of a carjacker waiting for a ride. Anyway, he took the money without saying thanks. At me he scowled, at Dushka he leered.

Dushka wanted to justify herself. "Really poor people have to wear all their clothes. I'm sure he had two jackets on. It's far too warm for two jackets."

"That's true," I agreed, because it was. It was also too warm for a fringed shawl.

"It meant more to him than to us, ten dollars."

"It's all right, Dushka."

In the restaurant she settled and became placid. When she turned her head, she did so slowly as if for a fashion shoot, showing every facet to the camera. I thought of the picture on her first CD. In it she is holding but not playing the violin, holding it by its neck. They had dressed and cinched her, so that her shape was congruent with that of the instrument. Her hair was arranged to fall Veronica Lake style over one side of her face. Nearest thing to kiddie porn.

"You'd better watch out," she said when I ordered something alfredo. "In spite of all you're running, you're getting fat."

I replied with a devil-may-care smile. "I eat what I like."

"Well, *I* can eat anything," she said, flipping her black hair with a starlet's nonchalance and looking around the restaurant.

"And yet you eat hardly anything."

Dushka straightened her back, raised her finger, and directed a sententious little speech at me. "What I choose not to eat is another matter entirely. Food isn't love and it isn't money either. Food's like music, like anything we take into ourselves to nourish our beings. I'm selective. It's a matter of taste."

I had heard this analogy between music and food before. "Do I love you because you repeat yourself, Dushka, or is it the other way around?"

"*I* repeat myself? You say you love me over and over. You say it all the time. Why is that? Repetition can be dangerous."

"I repeat it because it bears repeating."

She tilted her head. "Better an ox in a box than a hound in the pound."

"What's that? Another Slavic proverb?"

She raised a minatory finger. "New wine before old swill."

"Dushka?"

"Yes?"

"Do you miss it terribly?" To me the question sounded poignant, though perhaps not to her. It's true that repetition can be full of peril.

"What?"

I hesitated among two or three ways of putting it, this perennial question, another thing I could never stop myself from repeating. "You know."

She treated me to a semi-serious look, one not nearly so daunting as when she was sleeping or playing Sibelius.

"Sometimes I wonder if my career misses *me*. I imagine it wandering through the world—Leipzig, Amsterdam, Rio, London, Tokyo—hovering outside the Gevanthaus, sniffing the flowers in Covent Garden like a forlorn Dickens orphan looking enviously at the ample flesh of the cellists and the big shoulders of well-nourished percussionists, loitering by stage doors, wondering where, oh where on earth can little Dushka have gotten to. . ."

A set speech, delivered like a celebrity doing a magazine interview. But as my question had a subtext I persisted in my perversity. "No, really," I whispered.

"What?"

"*Do* you miss it?"

She put her elbows on the table and rested her chin on her little fists, patient with her impatience. "How many times do I have to tell you? I'm through with all that. Done. Burnt out. Kaput. Bobby Fischered. I'm glad I hung 'em up while I was still at the top, or at least in sight of it. . . Anyway, did I tell you about what Germaine's doing?"

This subject she always changes. "What's she up to now?"

"Writing a detective novel! Isn't it wonderful?"

"Wasn't Germaine taking sculpting lessons or something?"

"Oh, that was three months ago, and anyway it was aquarelle."

"*La dona e mobile.*"

"Well, she's a model, isn't she? She's admired for her looks."

"Does that explain anything?"

"Most everything, I should think. The eyes are appraising and the pressure's colossal."

"Worse than being a child prodigy? Well, Germaine's pretty enough, I suppose."

Dushka laughed. "She gets $2500 an hour. That's a pretty penny!"

"I do like her, you know."

"I know you try to, and you get credit for it. Most men don't really like Germaine. She scares them to death."

"Is that so? Well, yes, I can see how she might be intimidating." Of course, Germaine scared the bejeezus out of me.

"And yet she never—*almost* never—tries to do it. But it would be superhuman not to exercise the sort of power she has over men once in a while. Just for fun."

"She's flighty but she's interesting." I spoke like a wine connoisseur.

It was because they were both so interesting that Germaine and Dushka met. They were on a woman's TV talk show, a panel of successful young women. Dushka told me the main topic turned out to be eating disorders.

"Of *course* she's interesting. What could be more interesting than a supermodel with an I.Q. of 160? I mean, she's both beautiful and significant, like *la vie de Socrate.*"

"Pardon me?"

"Old stuff. The interesting is a border category, two things at once: in history a transitional period, in drama a rounded character. In Germaine's case it's those cheekbones and that brain."

"So," I said with a show of interest, "why a detective novel?"

"Apparently she read two of them on the red eye and thought she could do better."

"Did it ever occur to you what wonderful things Germaine might have achieved if only those famous cheekbones had been lower?"

Dushka began to cry.

"Don't cry."

"I can't help it. That poor history teacher. And poor Germaine too. Poor *everybody*."

I glanced around. "People are going to think I've just told you to get an abortion or something."

She looked up and very loudly declared, "You want me to get an *abortion*?" Heads turned.

"Look, I'm going to the men's room, Dushka. Stay put. If the waiter shows up just order some decaf for me, okay?"

"I want to go to the ladies."

"We can't both go."

"Why not?"

"It's an unwritten rule, like the law of the sea. Diners are forbidden to abandon their tables before the meal's over. Somebody always has to stay on the bridge."

Like a merry wave on a gravelly shingle, laughter broke over her tears. "Our table's a ship? Very well. If necessary, I'll go down with it."

How I loved her. No wonder I thought it bore repeating.

• • •

Like quite a few wealthy men, I became rich by accident; I mean, it happened while I was doing something else. In my case, prosperity was an unforeseen consequence of alienated tinkering. In my nerdy early years, I channeled teenage anomie into an obsession with the technology of the solitary, of those whose existence has always seemed to them virtual anyway. I fiddled with computers and one splendid week I put this device together. It worked just as I thought it would. It turned out that my little device made a lot of things possible that weren't before, many of which hadn't even occurred to me; yet these were just the sort of things people wanted to be possible the moment they found out they were possible, and things once not feasible become indispensable. As I fooled around, did I know how my device would be used? Was I even imagining a future that included it? Well, I suppose so, but in a sense so limited it scarcely counts. I was just a kid of nineteen, but not above being on the make. I found a good lawyer and we got an iron-clad patent and I held on to both the attorney and the patent until I was rich as Croesus, which, once the licensing agreements were signed, took all of about a year and a half. As they say, what a country.

When you hit the jackpot in your early twenties, you're supposed to give a ton of cash to your Mom and Dad. Basketball players do it. Actors do it. Dushka did it for a decade. You buy them houses and yachts and riding mowers. But my parents refused to take a cent from me which I regretted because, as my father surmised, I would have enjoyed gaining that stupid sort of advantage over him. They returned the Lexus I bought for them and sent back the cruise tickets. On the latter occasion, my mother wrote me a note explaining that she and Dad wanted for nothing, that of course they loved me dearly and desired to go on doing so (an unveiled threat!) and they were touched by my generosity. But the money, she let me know, was mine, not theirs, and they'd prefer to keep it that way. My dough, my responsibility, my fate.

I set up a scholarship at Columbia in their name, but my father demurred, and the fund wound up being dubbed for the device instead. Wise people, my parents, but not, in my opinion, big worriers about their little boy. They only began worrying about me after I got rich, as if I had suddenly become noteworthy the way somebody tied to railroad tracks might be. For a while they fretted about my marrying the wrong woman. Then, after some invisible transition, they worried that I might not wed at all. Mother told me flat out she regarded bachelorhood as even worse than a catastrophic marriage. For most of a year I let them wonder if their only child was gay, but in the end I answered the question without their having to ask. The truth was that they knew next to nothing about my emotional life—let alone my sexual one—because they couldn't bring themselves to inquire, and I told them nothing. Don't ask, don't tell was my house rule. And if silence failed, I simply lied.

They know nothing about Dushka.

• • •

Apart from the serious face, Dushka's sleeping habits are unpredictable. For example, she sleeps at irregular hours. When the Intermittent Sadness strikes her, she can spend an entire day in bed, yet I've known her to stay awake for forty-eight hours. Dr. Fein must at least have mouthed the word "bipolar" to himself when he heard these facts. Between Dushka and me, bedtime is a point of abrasion, a small protuberance but one where we rub up against each other three or four times a week.

I dread seeing Dushka reach for her violin case in the vicinity of midnight, especially when she hasn't played for a while. "My fingers," she'll say over her shoulder, panicked, "they're getting soft." Once, in sleepy foolishness, I suggested she might toughen her digits without actually bowing.

Dushka likes to begin with Bach, but she can wind up anywhere—Bartok, Kreisler, Gershwin, Hendrix (her own arrangement). I had the apartment soundproofed to mollify the neighbors, but this doesn't help me. So, when Dushka plays I read, filling in the canyons left by my unsatisfactory education, a process I began before Dushka moved in.

Impressed by a clever review a Berkeley English professor had written for the *Times*, I phoned him and asked for a reading list. The next day I sent him a check and my email address. Within the week I received an almost maliciously long alphabetized catalogue. I began with Aeschylus and six months later was only up to Baudelaire. That was when I met Dushka. In fact, the first night I spent with Dushka I read her Baudelaire, in my high-school French, and this is where her foot remark came from. It was quite a night: I'd read some Baudelaire, then she'd play some violin, back and forth till dawn. So, on our first night not only didn't we sleep together, we didn't even go to bed. It was a foretaste of many wee hours to come.

• • •

Dushka cries easily and when she does it's both my duty and my inclination to comfort her. But early on there was one night when Dushka made me cry. Then she was obliged to console me.

Having undertaken my musical education, she sent me out to buy a recording of *Die Winterreise*. I sat at her feet while she translated Müller's lyrics and explained how Schubert's music fitted into them. She spoke beautifully that night, but then about music Dushka never speaks other than beautifully.

"Most Schubert songs aren't built on contrasts, like Mozart's or Beethoven's, but on a kind of etching of the same line deeper and deeper," she explained. "It's what makes him a Romantic. Now, in this next song, *Die Post*, there *is* a contrast of themes, but this doesn't generate any heat. There's no proper resolution either. He just tamps down the vitality until there's only an *Abschied*. That means farewell. A goodbye to life itself I sometimes think. Now, pay attention."

Abschied. Dushka can make even German sound like love, whereas to me it usually sounds like murder. Her voice was balm to me, water on my parched senses. Maybe I didn't understand the music, but I understood Dushka.

Of Schubert's final song, *Der Leiermann*, she said, "Listen to how this repetition can break your heart."

I was happy yet I cried. It wasn't the heartbreaking *Die Leiermann* that made me weep. It was when Dushka told me about how young Schubert was when he died, only thirty-one. Love turned into death just like that. *Tod und das Mädchen.* I lay my head in her lap and she stroked my hair, like a mother.

Is it possible Dushka has stayed with me because I cried over Franz Schubert, because I was almost thirty?

• • •

Many hate, more fear, but in the end we all submit to dentists, lie beneath them belly up, like subordinating wolves.

The dentist of my childhood was Dr. Eberhard Gilroy, a huge figure of dread and authority. Though he ought to have retired years ago he still practices, and I still go to him. I believe everything he says, for Dr. Gilroy retails no opinions one could call casual. When I was a boy, he liked to talk digital computers with me; he encouraged me to work with them, promised it would pay off. A deep well of obiter dicta is Dr. G. "In local elections always vote for the party out of office." "Never tell a man he's gotten a good haircut or a woman that she's gotten a bad one." It's a wise man who can tell what's rotten from what's sound. Though his warnings about my mouth can be harrowing, I also find them reassuring. His warning that if I'm not careful I'll outlive my teeth implies that I'm going to live a long time. Anyway, opening wide for the dentist of your boyhood keeps you feeling young.

Dushka needed a good deal of dental work. Apparently, a lot gets neglected in the rearing of child prodigies. I took her to Dr. Gilroy, but she didn't care for the way he tsk-tsked over her. Still less did she like the catalogue of excavations and reconstructions he proposed to perform.

"He makes me sound like a public works project," she groused on the way home, "a *big* one. Horrible to lie there helpless while he pokes my gums and clucks his tongue like a nasty old hen. Do you ever watch his eyes? They're keen and bitter, always looking for signs of decay. He's spent decades doing that. Can't you see what it's done to him? No, I won't go back. I don't like your Dr. Gilroy."

"Oh, come now. I've known him all my life. He's a nice man."

"No," she insisted, shaking her head. "You shouldn't have taken me to him. He said I needed all these fillings and crowns. He hinted at bridges and root canals. When he finally took his fingers out of my mouth and let me speak, I asked him how many fillings *he* had."

I was interested. "You did? What did he say?"

"He didn't really answer. 'Oh, we dentists have a certain image to keep up,' is all he said. *Image*? Sadists with perfect teeth of their own, bicuspids that put their poor patients' to shame? No, I'm not going back to your dentist. He makes me think of Samson—the jawbone of an ass. It may be misplaced vanity, but I don't care for the idea that if I die in a plane crash the police would go to that man to figure out who I was." Finally, she put her finger in her mouth and mumbled plaintively, "He wants to drill me here, and here, and here, and way back here!"

So, I found another dentist for Dushka, a young Taiwanese woman. She and Dr. Deborah Wu have become fast friends, even though Dr. Wu also shot her full of x-rays and drilled her there, and there, and there.

One afternoon I returned from my checkup with Dr. Gilroy feeling displeased with both the dentist and myself because he said an old filling needed replacing. I found Dushka and Germaine in the living room. Dushka was on the floor, one spandexed leg over her head, while Germaine sat in serene perfection on the wing chair, Gloriana on her throne. Her long legs were crossed, her linen skirt was saucy, her blouse purple silk.

Dushka's voice was naturally a little strained. "Germaine stopped by; she's showing me some new yoga."

"Bonjour, Germaine." I couldn't help adding, "Showing?"

"I've been *describing* the exercises. Dushka's very good, don't you think? So flexible." She said this as if I might not have reason to know. If, in these, her salad days, Germaine was so waspish, what might she be like at forty? Her photogenic head inclined toward me, but her smile was not benevolent.

"So, you've been to the dentist. Full marks?" Germaine's English was learned from the English and her speech was full of phrases like *different to*, *full marks* and *it's early days yet.* I once heard her refer to a certain man's spouse as *the trouble and strife.*

Dushka chipped in too, as she bent her torso alarmingly to one side. "Gilroy building any bridges? Planning a coronation?" But then I could see she felt badly for me, as though she had taken Germaine's side. And what if Gilroy really had caused me pain? Dushka's empathy kicked in. It didn't console me. Dushka empathizes with everybody. "He didn't hurt you, did he?"

"No. I'm fine. Just need one filling replaced."

She got to her feet and turned to Germaine. "Remember? I told you about Dr. Gilroy. A brute, nothing at all like Deborah."

It appeared that Germaine had also become a patient of the sympathetic Dr. Wu. Three graces, norns, fates—weird sisters. I could imagine them drinking tea together and the picture was oddly disturbing.

"Deborah's so gentle, so sweet," Germaine declared complacently.

I went to the kitchen to get a soda. If the filling was bad, let it get worse. I needed to drive the dental taste from my mouth. The disintegrating filling had deprived me of that invulnerable feeling you get when you leave the dentist's office with a clean bill of toothy health. The women went on chatting: Dushka's voice full of enthusiasm, Germaine's delicately accented and attractive, though somewhat brittle and chilly, like shaved ice.

Germaine is certainly sharp, but I've often wondered about her brand of intelligence; that is, about how it works. My hypothesis is that she thinks primarily in images, in the way that mathematicians do in numbers, so swiftly that the images can pass for rational arguments. Where decay is concerned, Germaine's insights are as penetrating as a dentist's drill. Can the mind be twisted by the body's beauty? Could what Dushka called her power over men have made Germaine scornful? I remembered the detective story.

"How's the thriller coming?" I called in to Germaine.

"That's what we've been talking about," Dushka shouted back. "Germaine's hit on this wonderful plot. Come join us."

I set my soda on the coffee table. "Murder in a sealed room?"

Germaine laughed. "Nothing so hackneyed or contrived. My idea is to write a story that is entirely simple and banal on one level, but on another—that is, morally—rather complicated."

I lay down on the couch and put my feet up proprietarily. "I see," I said. "Realism."

• • •

It's a common error to believe that people feel the same way toward one another all the time. Like the atom, the heart is governed by a principle of uncertainty. For example, when I say I love Dushka, as I so often do, I'm not stating an absolute but a sort of probability. If you choose any random moment—and I believe even the most phlegmatic of us leads a mercurial emotional life—the odds are that what I would be feeling for Dushka would be love. On such odds we generalize. What else can we do? Purity is our ideal, but it exceeds our reach. Of course, I would prefer my love to be absolute. Indeed, it is—at times. But honesty demands I admit there are also moments, brief ones, when I do not love Dushka but hate her. It's no good claiming that hate is so mixed up with love that there's no difference, as if what mattered was only the spigot and not what's coming out of it. There are even occasions when I consider Dushka irrelevant to my life. This way I can pretend she's powerless to make me either happy or miserable. When she's in her oubliette of sadness, when she can't be reached and won't reach out to me, I feel rejected. So, I try to defend myself. But there's no relief in forced indifference; worse, there's a kind of deathliness about it. I soon go back to loving her. Love's like music and music's like food. Even ascetics get hungry.

I admit it: Dushka is my chief interest in life. What do I provide for her? Money, the condo, conversation, clothes, contributions to Amnesty International, attentiveness, solace, a dentist. But these are all *goods*. I fear I may be one of those ports of which any is welcome in a storm. Dushka adopted something of this attitude when she consented to live with me; there was no promise of permanence. She won't let me speak about marriage. She laughs and makes up Eastern European proverbs: "It's a fool who buys frayed rope." Dushka, who spent the second decade of her life hopping from one continent to another, incarnating the spirit of music, universally applauded, petted, toasted, acclaimed, whose life was a whirligig of concerts, recitals, hotel rooms, reception halls, tutors, and conductors, has come to me for a kind of quiet, a rest. For how long? *Haven*, it occurs to me, means harbor, and a harbor is only a temporary home. All my questions about her career really mean "Are you going to leave me?" And maybe her continual answer— "My career is over"—merely signifies, "No, I'll stay with you. . . for the time being. Better you should think that. Better I should, too." It's possible that my moments of not loving Dushka are at bottom practice for the day I discover her berth is empty. Any port in a storm means that, once the storm clears, one port's as superfluous as another.

• • •

"The story is quite simple," said Germaine. "My hero's name is Bolt. He's a private detective, so his work is chiefly about adultery and divorce. He's fortyish, divorced, childless, a solitary fond of the novels of Joseph Conrad and Scotch whiskey—single malt when he can afford it, anything else when he can't. Though he hardly has delicate scruples he is at base a decent man. Decency is what attracts him to Conrad."

"His or Conrad's?" I asked. I had read some Conrad because his name begins with C.

"Well, both."

"Does this Bolt like his work?"

"Not particularly, still it appeals to him. When he was seven, his mother discovered his father was bonking her hairdresser. A double loss for her. This event affected Bolt's view of married life. His own effort in that direction came a cropper in less than two years."

"Isn't that a little pat?"

"Of course, darling. It's fiction. *Popular* fiction, I hope."

"Go on."

"One day Bolt gets a letter on plain stationery with a goodish sized check. The letter is signed by Edward Dulac, but not the check. It is a bank check, made out to Bolt. Dulac explains that he suspects his wife and wants Bolt to spy on her. If his suspicions are borne out, he will expect a written report with photographs to be sent to him care of a firm of accountants, whereupon an identical bank check will be forthcoming. He gave his wife's name, Georgina, and their home address. Lastly, he forbade Bolt to contact him directly and on no account to telephone either his home or office."

"Seems relatively straightforward so far."

"Not at all."

"Why?"

Dushka grinned at my naiveté.

"Customarily," Germaine said patiently, "spouses come to see Bolt personally. They telephone and make appointments. They don't write letters. Suspicious husbands and wives are reluctant to write down their suspicions. Also, the check is rather odd. Why not a personal check?"

"Maybe his wife goes over the monthly statements."

"Possibly. But then there's the blank stationery with his home address written in. Why, no letterhead?"

"Well, it's a personal matter. If this Dulac's some sort of professional, I can see how he might feel funny about using office stationery."

"Yes, but why no request for Bolt to confirm that he's taken the case? In fact, why the warning not to contact him? It's all rather dodgy."

"All right. So Bolt's suspicious."

"Suspicious and perspicacious. But the money's good so he goes to work. Everything's easy enough, clockwork. He watches Dulac come and go to work, watches their boy come and go from school, stakes out Georgina for a fortnight, and discovers that she meets a man three times a week. They always have lunch at the same restaurant then go to a hotel for exactly two hours. He photographs them at both locations. By three-thirty she's back, a half an hour before her son arrives home from school."

"The child must be crucial for Bolt," said Dushka.

"Right," said Germaine.

"Reminding Bolt of his own ruined childhood?" Well, it *is* banal, I said to myself.

I watched Germaine talking, Dushka listening. They were both lovely women—but in such different ways! One of the first physical revelations I had about Dushka was that her body, which appeared so compact in public, could in private stretch into a whole landscape. Germaine, on the other hand, lacked any elasticity. It was as though she were made of some indestructible form of porcelain. I couldn't imagine her doing yoga. When Dushka first introduced me to Germaine I wondered if this perfect, self-contained creature could ever have fallen in love. Vulnerability on her part seemed unthinkable.

If Germaine appears immune to being hurt by life, Dushka's nerves lie just beneath her skin and sometimes one top of it. When she plays, for instance, they turn into four strings. Germaine's coolness emanates from a convincing carapace as if the woman were penetrated by a mask. However, I did once see Germaine *distrait*. At least I think I did. The moment was mysterious and unforgettable. It turned out to be a dangerous moment, sexy too. Germaine and I have been edgy around each other ever since, though not, I think, for the same reason.

It was a February day; a cold rain was falling. I bumped into her on the street. She looked harried and at first I thought she was simply wet and in a hurry. She kept touching her face and I thought she was anxious about her makeup. I stopped her. "Germaine," I said, "how are you?" and for a moment I could swear her eyes welled up. I'm sure it wasn't the rain. "Fine," she said with a tremor in her voice. Suddenly she touched me, a thing she had never done before and hasn't since. I always thought Germaine disdained human contact. She's not one to reach out, as Dushka does when she's not being intermittently sad. Perhaps Germaine believes that her touch is inflammatory, Midas-like. Anyway, she put her hand on my forearm. There was only the slightest pressure before she pushed off. It wasn't a squeeze, more like a bather touching the side of pool then pushing off. "Sorry, but I've got to rush off," she said, and did. That brief touch was electrifying though, the tiny, rounded pressure. For a second or two my head swam. It didn't occur to me that something unforgivable had happened.

I rushed home to Dushka and begged her to play something for me.

Germaine began to pontificate. "Detective stories are as much about innocence as guilt—more since in general there are at least half a dozen suspects and only one culprit. In fiction the detective's task is to restore order to the nursery, tidy up, sort things out. Bolt's job, however, is just the contrary. It's rare that he turns up innocence, rarer still that he leaves the scene in anything but turmoil and recrimination."

"This is a problem for Bolt?"

Germaine shrugged. "He likes Conrad, he identifies with Marlow, a man who cares about the proper stowing of ballast."

"So, what happens?" I asked.

Evidently, Germaine had told Dushka about most of the story, perhaps as much as she had written.

"Have you decided whether Bolt's going to send his report to Dulac?" Dushka asked eagerly.

Germaine leaned her head against the high back of the chair and narrowed her blue eyes.

"Bolt's in perplexity. He puts his report together, addresses the envelope, but he doesn't send it. He begins to think. He *deduces*. Bolt has a good head on him, but he seldom needs to use it. Now he does."

Dushka was resting her chin on her knees and looked pensively and touchingly young. "The heart never relents, does it?" she whispered.

This didn't sound like one of her proverbs. It upset me; I couldn't say why. After all, did I want the heart to relent?

Germaine continued. "Bolt turns over a notion he had entertained briefly at the outset, that his client might not be Edward Dulac. Now he considers more carefully. If the client isn't the husband, then who is he?"

Germaine paused, a piece of ironic dramatizing. She started to put her hand on Dushka's head, then drew it back. "What do *you* think, Dushka?"

Dushka took a moment to reply. "Well, there are several possibilities," she said. "For example, it could be somebody who's envious of the Dulac marriage and wants to break it up, maybe a jealous woman who covets Dulac for herself?" Her voice rose at the end of the sentence. I knew that quirk of Dushka's; making declaratives sound like questions meant she was feeling insecure.

Germaine dismissed this. "I'm surprised at you, thinking of a malicious *woman.* But as it happens Bolt does consider that possibility. He has enough misogyny to think the ploy is underhanded enough to be a woman's."

It was I who spoke up for womankind. "Why not a malicious man? Some enemy of Dulac's?"

"Don't you think such a man would simply confront Dulac with his information—or send him an anonymous letter? No, this was a person who wanted Dulac confronted with incontrovertible proofs, someone seeking both certainty and shock value."

"But then maybe it *was* Dulac," I said rather foolishly. "It's the most likely thing."

"Come now. That would hardly do for my story. Remember all those clues at the beginning? Didn't I say it would be morally complex?"

Germaine placed her palms on her Platonic thighs. "Earlier you made a joke. Murder in a sealed room."

"So?"

"It's the archetypal situation of the novel of detection. It isn't the murder that matters but the sealed room. The detective story is a closed form. Good ones have plenty of red herrings but no loose ends."

"I see!" cried Dushka.

I admitted I didn't.

"But how does Bolt figure it out, Germaine? *He* can't say it's because he's a detective in a story with certain conventions."

"It would make a change," Germaine laughed. "But no, you're right, of course. Bolt has to deduce the answer based on the evidence. You yourself hit on the critical clue when you said the child was crucial."

"Love can be so ruthless," Dushka murmured.

"Yes," said Germaine frigidly, as if love were some phenomenon she had learned about in a laboratory experiment.

The women were way beyond me. "I don't get it," I repeated grumpily. "Who's the client, then?"

"Think it through," said Professor Supermodel condescendingly. "The room has to be sealed and the child is the clue." She didn't wait for me to think. "Bolt, who of course has identified the lover, rings him up, insists on a meeting, says it's important. The lover refuses until Bolt suggests they lunch in the restaurant where he rendezvoused with Georgina Dulac. They meet the following day. Bolt orders a big meal and a shot of Laphroaig beforehand. The lover's nervous. Bolt produces an envelope, takes out the snapshots and his report. The lover glances at the pictures. 'You want money?' he says. 'But I already have your money,' says Bolt, 'though not the second payment, which I'm forgoing.

You can pick up the tab for lunch, though.' The lover looks so desperate that Bolt hesitates to tell him he intends to send his report to Georgina Dulac with a letter of explanation."

"A sympathetic bloke, your Bolt," said Dushka.

"Well, yes. But he's not sure where his sympathies lie," corrected Germaine. "He can't admire the lover's act, but he respects the depth of his motive. He's not sure whether he ought to side with Dulac or Georgina."

"Or the lover?" I asked.

Germaine delivered a non-sequitur that struck me as vicious. "I've made him a musician."

Dushka gave a start.

"So," I said with the stupid feeling you get when catching on a minute too late, "the lover hired Bolt to spy on himself, to expose the affair. Is that it?"

"Of course. What Bolt deduced was that the man loves Georgina and wants to marry her. Why won't she leave the dull husband? She can't love him, or she wouldn't be in that hotel three afternoons a week; besides, she adores music, and met her lover at a recital. So, is it the financial security or is she afraid of losing her son? Bolt would despise her if it were for the first reason, but, given his own childhood, he sympathizes with the second. Yet he also feels something for Dulac, not only because he looks like the only innocent party in the triangle, but also because of his own wife's infidelity. On the other hand, Bolt can't help wondering if Dulac may be unworthy of his sympathy. He may have driven Georgina into the musician's arms. Seated in the restaurant Bolt goes over all this in his mind. In fact, I plan to devote a quarter of the novel to Bolt's ethical analysis. To tell the truth, it's what most interests me. I'm going to call the book *Plane Geometry*."

I no longer believed Germaine was incapable of the pain of love, but it was clear to me that, even if she succeeded in finishing it, her Euclidean novel would never be published.

• • •

Dushka has not been the same since that afternoon with Germaine. Love is ruthless. The heart is relentless. The lover is a musician. He met his beloved after a recital.

I met Dushka at a reception after one of her recitals. I knew we would be introduced because I was the sole sponsor of the entire series. To tell the truth, I set the thing up to meet Dushka. Love is indeed relentless.

This was no longer the serious little girl who had played Sibelius. Before me stood a woman, young and nubile, but also on the point of utter collapse, as highly strung as her violin. The recital had gone badly. Dushka dropped notes, twice lost her place, and even I could tell that she was playing without conviction.

I talked her into letting me take her out for a bite. We went to La Mousse, where I had already made a reservation. I was witty, light-hearted; I made her laugh. Later on, at my place, I outdid myself, thanks to Baudelaire. I found verses for us:

Nous aurons des lits pleins d'odeurs légères,
Des divans profonds comme des tombeaux,
Et d'étranges fleurs sur des étagères,
Ecloses pour nous sous des cieux plus beaux.

There was even one for Germaine, in advance so to speak:

Je suis belle, ô mortels! comme un rêve de pierre,
Et mon sein, où chacun s'est meurtri tour à tour. . .

Dushka had her violin and wanted me to hear how well she could play, since I had heard her at her worst. After midnight she told it all, opened her heart. How her parents said she was their ticket out of wretched Bucharest, how they had driven and exploited her, the rootlessness of the last ten years, her weariness, the overwhelming urge she felt to stop performing.

She burst into tears. "I'm just another of those prodigies who outlive their talent!" We talked and talked. The suffering she had seen in her travels haunted her, she said. Life had lost its savor; the world was too cruel. Feeling lordly, I ordained a sabbatical for her. Her face lit up. My money smoothed the way. I sent a bundle of it to her parents and another to her manager. She became for me the extravagantly loved giantess Baudelaire imagined:

J'eusse aimé vivre auprès d'une jeune géante,
Comme aux pieds d'une reine un chat voluptueux.

• • •

Ever since that afternoon with the wicked Germaine, who will never pardon me for having seen her weep, Dushka has been practicing, four, five hours a day, as if she had been starving for the sound of her violin. My heart ached to see how her fingertips bled at first, but now they are as hard as molars. As for her playing, it is mature, profound, infused with her limitless compassion for hungry children, dissidents, imprisoned history teachers. All this playing makes me sad, and not intermittently. Dushka, though, is always happy now. It seems to me that her happiness was always curled up in her like a snake ready to strike me. She hasn't told me but I'm sure she's already phoned her manager. Dr. Wu has inserted the final crown. Perhaps the history teacher has been released. Even Schubert's death cannot help me. Already I can feel the emptiness, the *Abschied.* Every morning I wake up feeling as betrayed as Dulac, forlorn as Georgina's lover, forsaken as their child. The heart is relentless. Love may turn ruthless. Closed forms are disconsolate.

Larry's Complete Plumbing Service

I used to play tennis with Ernie Schwerin a couple weekends a month until we finally admitted that, whatever we were doing, it wasn't tennis anymore. After that, Ernie and I would meet for lunch from time to time and feast on foods outlawed by our wives and our doctors. Our breeze-shooting was desultory, without a lot of medical talk. Over a Reuben sandwich one Saturday, I bragged to Ernie that the next day I was going to install an overhead fan. I was practically rubbing my hands over the project. Now, to say I'm not handy would be putting it mildly, like describing the service in a French restaurant as a tad slow. Ernie knew that, like most unhandymen, I tended to deny what had been amply demonstrated. He was the kind of doubles partner who never complained when you double-faulted or served one to the back of his head. Ernie's a forbearing guy, sensitive to the feelings of others. He spared mine about the overhead fan by making fun of himself as an indirect way of giving me sound advice. "You know," he said as he picked up the second half of his corned beef on light rye, "experience has taught me that my best home improvement tool's my checkbook."

I recalled this dictum when my wife made the same point more directly. This wasn't after I'd failed for weeks to fix the running toilet in the powder room or to stop the faucet in the upstairs bathroom from dripping. She held off until I was making ready to tackle whatever was keeping the kitchen sink from draining.

"Damn it, George. Stop being pig-headed and just call a plumber," she said brutally. "Honest to God, I don't know which is worse—your cheapness or your overconfidence."

That hurt, I'll admit. I didn't like having both my manhood and generosity challenged, razed to the ground, even by a woman I'm pretty sure loves me for my many faults as well as my few virtues. Then I remembered Ernie. *He'd* have phoned a plumber and this, I felt, gave me permission to call in a pro. Consoled by the solidarity of incompetence, I told my sensible wife I'd do what she told me to.

"Good," she said. "I'm going shopping with Brenda."

I went online to look up local plumbers. I didn't like the guy who came when the hot water heater spewed all over the basement. He had me over a barrel and charged accordingly.

Larry's Complete Plumbing. New business. Introductory offer. All work 25% off. 24-hours.

The home repairs website gave Larry five stars and offered three testimonials.

-Quick and reasonably priced.

-Good work. Fair price. Polite. Friendly.

-We had five house guests for the holidays, and somebody put in something they shouldn't so our toilet backed up on Christmas morning. Larry was here in half an hour and fixed it. The man's a saint.

Saints go by their first names, but plumbers usually favor their last ones. Larry. A man willing to give his first name to the job. And at a discount.

I phoned and got an answering service, apparently a teenager. She asked me to please wait a moment while she could "like check Larry's schedule." I got thirty seconds of Vivaldi, which felt like another good sign.

"He can be there in like an hour?" she said. "That okay?"

"Most satisfactory," I said dryly and gave her (like) my name and address.

Fifty minutes later Larry was at the door. He wore khaki overalls, had his toolbox in hand, a Red Sox cap on his head, and a gentle smile on his face. There was something familiar about his face; it took me half an hour to figure out what and, even then, I could scarcely believe it. During that half-hour, Larry put a new flapper in the downstairs head, a washer in upstairs faucet, and, after diagnosing the problem, snaked the kitchen drain until it ran like Niagara during a wet spring.

I'm what's called a lapsed Catholic which, in my case, is somebody who went to church and took CCD classes until he got old enough not to. My wife goes to mass twice a year, Christmas and Easter—she calls it her "fix". I think it's more about nostalgia than faith. If she ever goes to confession, I don't know about it. I pay far less attention to the Church than I do to the Sox, Pats, Celts, and Bruins. But you didn't have to be any kind of Catholic at all to have been riveted by the story coming out of Rome a couple years back. Two stories, actually: the choice of the first (probably last) American pope and then his resignation. Laurentius the First. Laurentius the Last.

Larry the plumber? Laurentius the ex-pope? Ludicrous, but he was a dead ringer. Just take off the ballcap, put on a white zucchetto, substitute robes for overalls and there he'd be. Was it possible?

I was sitting in the living room mulling over this question while Larry cleaned up the kitchen floor and packed up his tools. Then he was standing in the hall just outside the living room, avoiding the carpet with his work boots.

"All done, George. It was George, wasn't it?"

"Yep." I got up to take a close look at him.

"How's a hundred bucks sound?" Larry asked.

Now, would a pope—even an American one—say "a hundred bucks"? For that matter, would a pope—even an ex one—be fixing sinks and toilets? Still, the closer I looked, the surer I got.

"You're *him*, aren't you?"

He looked theatrically puzzled. "*Him*?"

"Laurentius the First."

His face fell.

"You mean nobody's noticed before?"

"Nope."

"And you'd have preferred it if I hadn't either. Right?"

"Right."

"Sorry. Too late."

"Too bad."

"Look," I said, naturally excited, "do you have to go *right* away?"

With a deep sigh he took his cell phone from the pocket of his overalls. I expect he'd have liked to lie and make a quick getaway. But he hadn't even been able to lie about being the ex-pope, which, given the odds, I'd have accepted.

"Not for an hour."

"Then how about I get us a couple of beers and write you a check. I've got pizza slices in the freezer. Good stuff. Bertucci's. Pepperoni. One minute in the microwave. What do you say?"

Larry rubbed nervously at his thigh. It was as if I was holding a gun on him.

"Look," he said, "can you, you know, just keep it to yourself. I'm trying to make a fresh start here. The press—"

"Say no more, Your Quondam Holiness. I get it. So, pizza and beer? I mean, it's not bread and wine, but still."

"Seriously? You're going to make jokes?"

"Sorry again. Forgive me, Fath. . . Oops. Okay. Come on, let's go into the kitchen. We'll eat and chat and I'll write that check."

"You've got questions, don't you?" he said anxiously.

"Sure. Some. I'm the curious type. And I guess neither of us goes to church for our answers these days."

I did have questions even though coverage of Larry's resignation had saturated the planet for almost a month. I remembered, in a vague sort of way, that he grew up poor somewhere in New York's classical belt, felt a vocation, became an outstanding parish priest, worked with the hungry and homeless, spoke with eloquent simplicity that led to comparisons with the Master of Parables. He was popular, appeared on TV, was talked about, taken up by Cardinal O'Hara. He became the country's youngest bishop, spent a year in the Vatican carrying out various bureaucratic tasks, making contacts and learning the ropes. The old pope took to him and made him a cardinal. After a reported thirty-four-vote deadlock in the Sistine Chapel, his election astonished everyone but, according to his first public speech, no one more than himself.

He threw himself into the job. If young and energetic is what the College of Cardinals wanted, it's what they got. He had ideas for reforms and wasn't slow to act on them. He retired a hecatomb of deserving bishops, defrocked a score of child-abusers, hired Deloitte to do an outside audit of the Institute for the Works of Religion, aka the Vatican Bank. There was resistance aplenty, especially when he put priestly celibacy and the ordination of women on the table.

I remembered my wife showing me an article about the new pope's troubles. The Curia was resisting just about everything he wanted to do. The Hierarchy grumbled about a colossal mistake having been made, and there was plenty of sneering at "American notions." According to a breathless article, which I thought belonged more in

People magazine than *The National Catholic Reporter*, there were palace intrigues, rumblings of a coup.

Then, suddenly, just a year into his papacy, Laurentius the First announced his resignation, not only from the throne of Peter but from the Church, from Roman Catholicism. He was swiftly replaced by Cardinal Cazares, the feisty Spanish conservative whose all-too-predicable nickname was Torquemada. Cazares took the papal name Pius XIII, tying himself, as the press noted, to Piuses XI and XII who had managed to get on with Mussolini, Franco, and Hitler. Several liberal reporters took pleasure in reminding their readers how thirteen became an unlucky number.

Meanwhile, the former Pope Laurentius came home, granted one evasive interview to the *New York Times,* then hid from the press. Before long, the Church moved back and the world moved on.

Larry drank his Bass ale straight from the bottle. "All right," he sighed like a trapped man making the best of it. "What do you want to know?"

"Why Laurentius? I mean, I don't suppose Larry's your real name so why Laurentius?"

"To honor John XIII, actually. I was a big fan."

"I don't get it."

"John was a progressive, but he honored traditions too, even obscure ones. You've heard of anti-popes?"

"Something to do with Avignon, wasn't it?"

"Started much earlier, almost from the beginning of the Church. Different factions, different popes. A serious threat to the doctrine of apostolic succession. The original John XXIII was a Pisan anti-pope. The second one cancelled him out by taking his name. Magical thinking, I know, but touching. Well, there was another anti-pope called

Laurentius. He held the throne for nearly a decade."

"When was that?"

"From 498 to 506. CE, of course."

"So, you cancelled him out?"

"Theodoric forced him out of office but, yup, I cancelled him. Old news."

"*Really* old."

"The Church has a long memory."

"And is that why you're Larry now?"

He shrugged. "One name's as good as another when you want to disappear with an alias. I liked the irony. From Laurentius on one sort of throne to plain old Larry fixing another kind. Next."

"What did you live on when you came back home? Where was it? Utica?"

"Troy actually."

"Well, I don't suppose you got a pension, or even severance. So, what did you do for money?"

"I had some savings and a small pension from my pre-pontifical work. It was cut but not to nothing. Anyway, I didn't need much. Rents are low in Troy. There are plenty of unemployed men and I was just another one. Next."

"Okay. So far as I know, nobody ever nailed why you did it. So, what *was* it? Resistance to your reforms? The umpteenth bank scandal? The child-abuse? A bridge too far with celibacy and women priests?"

He gave me a wry smile. "None of the above. Want another guess?"

"Nope. So, what was it, then?"

"Simple. I lost my faith and with it my occupation."

I looked at him hard. "Wow. Imagine. The Pope."

"It was one of those massacres of the innocents. Toddlers, babies, infants. Christianity began with a slaughter of babies and ended with the sacrifice of a son. The whole of monotheism began with Abraham prepared to kill Isaac. It all tumbled down for me. I re-read Augustine and couldn't buy it. Not the theodicy with God bringing good out of evil; not the free will business either, with God knowing what we're going to do before we're even born. Augustine was attempting to square circles, trying to reconcile an omniscient, omnipotent, all-loving God with murdered babies. It's all deductive reasoning. Since God's perfect therefore. . . and so on. I knew the argument, that we're too limited and dumb to understand the divine plan. Worse, Augustine put blind faith before reason, even said you couldn't know anything without it. That move clogged scientific progress up for a thousand years, just like orange peels and hairballs did your kitchen sink. I lost it. Zap. After that, I didn't really have a choice."

"I guess I can see that."

"I'm glad."

"So, why *here*? Why *this* town?"

"I was tracked down in Troy. The South was out. I don't like heat and humidity. Rome in summer is insufferable. So, I did some research. This town used to be full of the faithful—Irish and Poles mostly. I'm sure you've noticed how the local Catholic schools and churches have been turned into condos and old folks' homes."

"Everybody said it was the abuse scandals. A short ton of last straws."

"Right." He looked at his watch. "Look, I've really got to go."

"One last question."

"If I answer it, you'll keep your mouth shut about what Larry the plumber used to do for a living?"

"Cross my heart. I'll give you a sparkling review on Yelp, and I won't even tell the wife."

"Never been married, of course, but I'm guessing that's not so easy."

"True. But not impossible."

"Okay, shoot."

"Why *plumbing*?"

He chuckled. "Before I went into the seminary, I worked a couple of summers with my Uncle Brian. He was a master plumber and said I had a real knack for the work. I liked it too. Plumbing's not exactly a religious vocation, of course, but it is a kind of calling. Anyhow, after I came back, a friend arranged for me to become the oldest plumber's apprentice in all of Rensselaer and Oneida counties. I worked and studied and, in the fullness of time, got my license."

"So, from poping to plumbing, then?"

"Fitting, don't you think?"

"How?"

Larry stood up and I heard in what he said an echo of the celebrated eloquence of his old homilies and edicts and bulls.

"From the airless, empty heights of a depopulated heaven to the solid, lowly, earthy level of the drains. From nine species of angels and countless saints and martyrs to the stopped-up pipe under your kitchen sink. Not a pretty thing, a clogged drain, but incontestably real.

Sometimes what looks like a step down can be a step up."

I've thought a good deal about what Larry meant by down and up, the directions on which he was briefly the Church's final arbiter. If he meant what I think he did, I'm glad, even, in a way, consoled.

I've kept my promise. It hasn't been hard. My wife wasn't curious about the plumber, just over the moon to have everything working again. During a lull in one of our luncheon chats, I was tempted to tell Ernie Schwerin; but I persuaded myself that he wouldn't believe me anyway. However, if he ever needs a plumber, I've got my recommendation ready.

Are You A Good Witch Or A Bad Witch?

After the tragedy, I tried three times to talk to Betty though what I really longed for was to hug her. I ached to sob with her, to give and take comfort. For thirteen years, we were best friends, but she wouldn't even look at me and, when last I saw her in the garage and ran toward her with my arms open, she stepped back and hissed, "Get off me," as if I'd dared to touch her.

This afternoon, Cecile Glatthorn, assuming I must know or spitefully pointing out that I didn't, asked me where Betty's moving. When I said I'd no idea, that I didn't know she was moving, her eyebrows went up. "Really?" Then she gave her head a sad little shake. "Too many memories of Charlotte, I suppose?"

It seemed to me Cecile made it a question in the hope that I'd admit that Betty was moving to get away from me. I don't know how much of the story Cecile knows. She's not a bad person, not a terrible gossip, just a woman with a compulsion to know other people's business. It's not unlikely that she was jealous of my closeness to Betty, felt shut out, or maybe she just noticed that we stopped seeing each other and wanted to find out why.

So, Betty is moving away. Now she won't have to squeeze past me in the elevator, evade me in the parking garage. She won't have to see me anywhere, at any time, ever again.

When he was six my big brother Joe dressed up as G. I. Joe, then as Superman for three Halloweens in a row. He loved running in his cape, making muscles, squinting as he focused his super-vision and super-hearing.

After I saw *The Wizard of Oz*, I didn't want to be Dorothy for Halloween; I wanted to be Glinda. My costume turned into a family project. Mother got a length of pink cloth and made a replica of Glinda's gown with those winged power shoulders. Father strung together chicken wire to hold the skirt out in a hoop then made a high crown out of cardboard, aluminum foil, and rhinestones. He was so proud of that crown that I think he'd have been glad if I never wore it. As for my brother, he went into the woods and came back with the perfect stick for my wand. He sawed it to length, whittled it down, and sanded it smooth. "I want superpowers too, witch powers," I confided to him, and he said, "Sure. Why not?" As Joe had pretended to see through walls, I pretended I could read people's minds and look into their future. I boasted to my friends that I could do these things—semi-seriously—and they played along. I remember Marjorie asking if I could change people into animals, "You know, like the way Circe turned men into pigs." And then Jeannie made us laugh. "Don't bother," she said as if she knew more than she did. "Boys do that all by themselves."

It was a game at first, but then I began to half-believe I really had these powers. If I concentrated, I sometimes got a sense of what people were thinking; it was usually muddled but not always. I got a feeling for what lay in store for them too, not anything specific, only whether it would be good or bad, as if life were a trek between crossroads. Perhaps these "powers" would have gone away if Joe had mocked, if my friends hadn't played along. "What's Billy Fratangelo thinking about?" or "Should I go to my aunt's on Saturday or to the mall with you?" They were kidding but at the same time they really wanted me to answer. And sometimes I was right. I'd get these sensations about what was going to happen—apprehension, excitement, joy, dread. And these feelings, these powers or illusions, didn't diminish as I got older; I didn't grow out of them. On the contrary.

When I told Joe about my predictions and mind-reading, he didn't make fun of me even though it was he obvious didn't believe any of it—or perhaps I should just say Joe believed in my powers less than I did. I think he didn't discourage me because he wanted me to give up what might become a delusion on my own. So, every now and then—when we'd be talking about getting into college, some girl he liked, or the rock group I was into—he'd go silent for a moment then suddenly challenge me.

"Okay, tell me what I'm thinking about *right now.*"

I'd close my eyes and pretend and not pretend to concentrate.

"What every boy your age thinks about at least twenty times an hour," I said.

"You're blushing!"

"Am not."

"Then you've just developed one awful rash."

When Joe was a senior, he asked me about his girlfriend, Brenda, who was a junior.

"Will she dump me when I go away to school?"

I wasn't in doubt. "Yep. I'd say you can count on it."

Joe said, "You're kidding, right?" but he frowned. People are always more likely to believe bad predictions than good ones.

Brenda aside, Joe had a choice to make. He could go to Carnegie-Mellon, the University of Illinois, or West Point. He'd always loved military history. He had the grades for the Academy, and he was in great shape, starring on the gymnastics squad for three years. In fact, it was his gym coach, a veteran, who told him he should apply to West Point. They admitted him. G. I. Joe. He suffered through a week of indecision. He listened to our parents go back and forth for days before he turned to me.

"Well, what do *you* think?"

I told him he should go to West Point. I said he'd have a brilliant military career.

He did go to the Academy and his career was brilliant, for a while. He finished eighth in his class, aced Ranger training, was promoted from second lieutenant to first and captain in record time. Then, on a night mission in Iraq, my big brother was shot to pieces.

While I'm not puke-green-Margaret-Hamilton ugly, I'm a long way from Melissa Joan-Hart and Elizabeth-Montgomery pretty. The good looks went to Joe. So, I haven't lived my life besieged by beaux. In high school, kids traveled in loose clumps more than pairs. This suited me because I could usually secure a place on the periphery of the popular scrum. It was almost like belonging. I had plenty of girlfriends to invite me along because I was a useful foil; I made the better-looking look better. Then came college.

I chose Champaign-Urbana chiefly because Joe didn't. Social life was different there, all about pairing-off. The anxious scent of husband-hunting wafted through the women's dorms; wedlock was romantic culmination to some, market transaction to others—and both at once for those with scope and irony, all the Jane Austen fans. I had a few dates and only two boyfriends at UI. Gregory Schultz was in my calculus class, at the head of it while I was at the foot. Shy, spectacled, whip-smart, and defensively sarcastic, I found Gregory's mind far easier to read than Rudin's *Principles of Mathematical Analysis*. It seemed to me mostly a jumble of short-lived, incisive perceptions all tangled in a yarn-ball of self-doubt. Two of his thoughts came through vividly on our fifth and last date though, as our clothes were coming off. First, *Jesus, what if she gets pregnant?* Second, *She might be the best I can do.*

In a clean anti-mathematical sweep, I dropped Gregory Schultz and Calculus 110 at the same time. For the rest of the semester, Gregory sent me witty and whining emails that all ended with his asking why I broke up with him. That was sophomore year.

The next year I was introduced to Jude Matlaw, an entirely different animal. He was just about perfect and appeared to think I was, too.

Jude stood six-feet tall, was left-handed, level-headed, modest, wiry, kind, and a senior. He was pre-law, majoring in history. He liked fly-fishing, basketball, poetry, the works of Barbara Tuchman and David McCullough, French New Wave cinema, Kansas City barbecue, and me. His mind was lovely to look into, like the paneled reading room at the Library, neat and masculine, polished wainscoting, lots of tall windows and a twenty-foot ceiling. We saw each other from November, when we were introduced at a mixer, through the spring, when he got his acceptance to Columbia Law. We celebrated with a banquet at the Omega Diner and then went for a stroll in the soft air and light of the April evening. We were walking by Boneyard Creek when he suddenly popped the question, sort of.

"Will you wait until I finish law school?"

"For what?"

"To get married, of course."

I threw my arms around him and said yes, yes, of course.

We had a week together in July and spent half of it finding him a place to live in Manhattan and the other half in the Quahog Inn on Cape Cod

When school started, Jude set up a schedule. He promised to phone every other night at ten o'clock. During one call, as he was telling me about torts, I tried to grasp what was going on in his mind, which was usually like a filing cabinet. What I glimpsed was like two snapshots. While listening to him drone on about liability cases, I got an image of a good-looking redhead with a serious face and smooth hair. She was pulling her blouse over her head. In the second image, she was naked, belly down, on a bed.

I interrupted Jude's lecture and asked him if there were any redheads in his Torts class.

"I don't know what you're talking about," he said quickly, a dead giveaway that he did, exactly what perps say to the cops on tv.

Then we argued.

Then we broke up.

And that was that. I mean, that was *really* that.

So, I'm single and childless, just like that poor old cannibalistic crone in her gingerbread house in the forest.

After dropping calculus, I gave up being pre-med and decided to major in French. That's how pendulums work. I'd liked French in high school, enjoyed books by Gide, Colette, Duras, and loved Godard and Truffaut's movies. My mother and I watched *The French Chef* together, tried the recipes and shouting "Bon Appetit"; and, well, the whole idea of Frenchness appealed to me. For the subject of my senior thesis, my advisor suggested Lucie Delarue-Mardus, who wrote far more than I was prepared to read, more, in fact, than she should have—seventy books.

Impractical degree in hand, I moved to Chicago where all I could find was waitressing jobs. Then I had an idea. When they got over my asking for more money after all they'd laid out the four years at UI, my parents advanced me the tuition to enroll in Robert Morris University's secretarial program, the best in town. I promised I'd pay them back. I loved the training; I really took to work I found exacting but not demanding. I was sure I'd found my *métier*, my *niche* (two fine French words). The orderliness and neatness of secretarial work satisfied me, and the limited demands were soothing. The prospect of serving others with complete emotional detachment attracted me too. I even liked my teachers' trivial hints: fold any paper you toss away so it'll take up less space in the wastebasket; never ever show up for work bearing cookies. I felt confident that I'd be worth something on the market.

Electronics Corporation of Chicago, ECC, hired me. I started, of course, at the bottom, in the *pool*, though they didn't call it that. When I dared to try them, my powers came in handy. I had a knack, my bosses said, for knowing what they wanted before they did. If I saw one of them was about to make a mistake, I learned to give an indirect warning: "Are you quite sure about that, Mr. Sterling?" I folded what I didn't shred, never brought cookies, and moved up rank after rank, just as my brother had. When the CEO's longtime executive assistant retired, HR sent me to be interviewed. I had a good feeling about how it would go, and I got the job. Before long, Mr. Barthelemy was introducing me as "the pin in the pinwheel," as if he hadn't hired but invented me. Praises and raises have not been lacking. "I don't want to lose you," he said when giving me a whopping increase. "It's as if you can read my mind."

I saved up, paid my parents back, and made the down payment on my big two-bedroom condo on North Wells Street. I moved in three months before newly divorced Betty and seven-year-old Charlotte moved in one floor up. Betty was an anesthesiologist, and Charlotte was adorable. That first night I brought them a Julia-style pot roast with bliss potatoes, parsnips, carrots, and green beans.

Betty had more of a social life than I did—who didn't? Also, she was sometimes called to the hospital for emergencies. One night, desperate because her regular sitter wasn't available, she phoned to ask if I could possibly stay with Charlotte. She thought it might be for a couple of hours, maybe three.

I brought up the makings for macaroni and cheese and my DVD of *The Wizard of Oz*. Charlotte was easy to love. There was nothing mean about the child, nothing but sweetness and worries that did her credit and which I liked relieving. Over time, as Scrooge was to Tiny Tim, I thought of myself as a second mother to Charlotte. She popped into my place whenever she liked, for talks and treats. We binged together on Disney movies. I taught her some French—*nous sommes les meilleurs amis, n'est-ce pas?*—and, when she had to pick a foreign language in middle school, *naturellement* she chose French. I gave her two books by Colette for her fourteenth birthday. We watched

Restless and *Band à part*. Charlotte told me things she said she couldn't tell her mother and I never once betrayed her confidence. She worried about Betty being lonely and she missed her father; later, it was grades, hair, thighs, and boys. Lots of boys were interested in Charlotte. And so it went for a decade.

Betty was devastated when Charlotte went off to Tufts. For three days she went sort of mad. I wasn't much better, to tell the truth. Betty and I talked every night and maybe that helped us, the consolation of feeling the same things.

Charlotte phoned home regularly and sent me weekly emails, some of them quite long. Betty got the big, redacted picture while I got the details. In one email, Charlotte said she was feeling depressed and didn't know why, since things were going very well. I phoned her because I thought if I could hear her voice, I might be able to see into her mind. And it was true—at least I thought it was. She was just blue; it wasn't anything serious. Anxiety, self-criticism, a little homesickness, feeling like the East might not be for her. I told her a French joke and was pleased to hear her giggle.

Though I never shared with Betty all I knew about Charlotte, I did tell her everything about myself. She was my one confidante, as my brother once was. She knew about Joe and about Jude. I even told her about my "powers," which amused her. She didn't ridicule me, but she was, after all, an unmetaphysical physician. When I beat her at gin rummy or Scrabble, she'd tease me about reading her mind.

Charlotte had a string of boyfriends during her first two years at Tufts, none serious. But in her junior year, she fell in love. His name was Geoffrey Longacre, an economics major from Westchester county and money. He took her on expensive dates in Boston. I learned a lot from her emails about Beantown gastronomy, concerts, and theater. For Thanksgiving, she went to Westchester. The visit went well. Geoffrey's family welcomed her warmly, and their golden retriever would hardly leave her side.

Betty went to Boston for a weekend early in November to meet Geoffrey. She was favorably impressed, took lots of pictures, and gave me a complete rundown when she got back. Geoffrey was handsome, polite, and obviously—Betty said "spectacularly"—enamored of Charlotte. All good.

I met Geoffrey when he and Charlotte came home for Winter Break. I was invited to dinner on Christmas Eve. I felt uneasy from the first. It wasn't that I didn't like the young man or that I found anything disturbing about him, in his mind—nothing beyond some understandably risqué images of Charlotte. It was sensing something about the future that shook me. It wasn't specific but it was definitely bad. Something terrible would happen if the couple married; that's what I felt. I did my best to dismiss my uneasiness and couldn't. It kept me up that night and was even worse when I went upstairs to deliver presents the next day. I told myself that I was wrong, denied my "powers," chided myself for indulging an old delusion. But the dread only deepened.

I knew I was on thin ice and told myself to keep my mouth shut, that it wasn't really any of my business. Anyway, what could I say that wouldn't be dismissed and resented? I was in anguish but also perplexed. Geoffrey Longacre was a fine fellow; he and Charlotte were in love and could look forward to a happy future. Though I knew Betty thought her daughter too young to marry, she didn't make an issue of it. My dread was a certainty wrapped up in uncertainty. My feelings grew worse until I was filled with inexplicable horror.

In the end, I had to tell Betty, to warn her.

"What are you talking about?"

"I don't know what, not exactly. I just *feel* it."

Betty grew angry, then furious. "It's that crazy fantasy of yours. The crazy witch business, isn't it?" she scoffed.

"What can I do? You've got to believe me."

It was terrible, Betty's face, what she said.

"*Believe* you? Believe in a neurotic delusion you've been cultivating your whole empty life? Believe in some hallucinations that make you feel better about yourself, that you're special?" She looked at me with disgust, without pity. "Don't you see what's going on here?"

"What do you mean?"

Then it poured out.

"Joe and Jude. Especially *Jude*. You're jealous of Charlotte. She's got what you threw away. And not only that. You've always been jealous of me *because* of Charlotte. Admit it. You've wanted to take her from me with your little confidences. Oh, I know all about them. I indulged you and so did Charlotte. We'd laugh about it. But this is too pathetic. *You're* pathetic. The bad fairy at the feast."

"No, no. Don't say that. It's what I feel. I can't explain."

"Don't bother trying. Just leave."

I wasn't invited to the wedding. Charlotte, informed by Betty, didn't reply to my emails. I was now the bad fairy, the wicked, envious, lonely, barren witch.

Horribly ironic that Betty, so level-headed, so grounded, so sensibly dismissive of my "powers," should hold me responsible for what happened, as if it were my doing, the fulfilment of a spiteful wish.

The couple honeymooned in the Bahamas. I only found out where they'd gone when the tragedy hit the news. Betty didn't tell me, didn't come to weep with me. I saw the story on television. Charlotte and Geoffrey—a vibrant, joyful wedding picture on the TV—drowned while skin-diving.

What was it? Bad scuba gear? Some sex thing? Rapture of the deep? The authorities, said the announcer, were investigating.

And what was I? And who would investigate me?

I'll Never Know

Parents are a given for most children, two unchosen facts of life, like the kitchen clock and the bedroom wallpaper. But there must be some children, like me, who are mystified by their parents, especially by how they ever came to be married. By the time I was an eight-year-old, having observed familiarity without affection and dependency without warmth, I concluded Mother and Father were ill-matched, that somebody at the wedding should have leapt up and spoken rather than forever holding their peace. The wedding guests weren't many or likely to leap. I've seen the faded Polaroids. There were my two widowed grandmothers, a brace of aunts and one uncle, three young cousins, and hardly any friends. Everybody looked at the camera with the same fixed grin, inverse of the fixed frown deployed at funerals. In their formal portrait, Mother stood to the left of the wedding cake in her plain white dress. She had the wan smile of a reluctant bungee-jumper who'd just decided to take the dare. To the right of the cake, Father appeared pleased with himself, the way he used to after checking some chore off his list. The focus of the picture is really the wedding cake.

I've often wondered about their courtship, whether they were briefly infatuated, deluded, tired, or terrified of winding up single. Neither would tell me much about their dating beyond that they were fixed up on a blind date. As for the rest, they might as well have forgotten. I could be sure that they engaged in sexual relations at least once, but, as an only child, I couldn't be certain that they'd done it twice.

As mothers go, mine was dutiful but undemonstrative, a constant but passive presence in our semi-detached house. The blue-gray wallpaper in what had once been my nursery had a repeating pattern of an airplane, train, and ocean liner, all of them streamlined, in the style of the 1930s. Like the wallpaper, I would have missed my mother if she weren't there.

Like the speeding plane, train, and liner, Mother might have been seething with potential energy, with dreams of travel and escape, but she didn't move. She was more like my father's hired housekeeper than his beloved helpmate, a timid cook and cleaner with an inclination toward agoraphobia. Did we love each other? Yes, in a firm but abstract way, founded on the fact that she was the mother and I was the child.

It was my father who generated the weather in the house—his moods, ideas, weariness, irritation, sobriety, boredom, and exaltation. He was a pharmacist who owned his own store, wore a white lab coat at work and wielded the dual authority of science and business. He was dissatisfied with himself because being a pharmacist lacked the dignity of being a physician, physicist, or chemist. Running a drug store that stocked candy bars, comic books, and under-the-counter condoms hardly made him a captain of industry. Once—it was when he was driving me to my interview at the university he'd attended—he let slip that as a freshman he had aimed for medical school. I wanted to ask if he'd flunked Chemistry 101 but didn't dare.

Father was sensitive about his status. He had the anxiety of the middle of the middle class, aspiring to move up, afraid of slipping down. Perhaps that's why he wanted me to excel, to distinguish myself, to be impeccable in my deportment, to make not merely prudent decisions but wise ones. There was some vision of excellence in his mind which I was to fulfill and which he ceaselessly admonished me to follow; but this pattern wasn't himself. He was no paragon, no celebrity winner of awards. He was not famous—but someone else was.

The Author haunted my childhood and pervaded my adolescence, a god dictating commandments like Moses' and, like Mohammad's, speaking through his messenger. Father was this distant deity's secretary and prophet.

I heard early and often how, as a freshman, my father made friends with a classmate who lived in the dorm room next to his. On the way to my interview, I heard it again.

"We couldn't stand our roommates—shallow, crude, rowdy eighteen-year-olds angling for bids from the popular fraternities. We bonded, ate together, talked past midnight, traded books, disparaged or idolized professors, critiqued the school's social structure, chewed over all the big questions you ask at that age. We were close for all four years. And we still are. We correspond regularly."

The Author was a history major. He already knew French and Latin and took up Greek his first year. He made Phi Beta Kappa, graduated *Summa cum Laude* with a Woodrow Wilson Fellowship. He started graduate school but dropped out when his first novel was a sensation. That brief bildungsroman was assigned in my eleventh-grade honors English class. My father beamed when I told him, beamed the way he didn't in the wedding portrait.

"I can't stress this enough," he said to me during my senior year. "It's extremely important to make good friends in your college years, *superior* friends."

Father wasn't talking about useful contacts or networking. He meant I should make a friend like the Author—that is, somebody who would ascend into the firmament.

The Author never visited us but, every summer for five or six years, my father locked up the store, packed a bag, and headed off for a long weekend with the Author in the Green Mountains. Mother and I were stranded without the car.

The first such trip came when I had just started high school. Father came back excited.

"He has a big white farmhouse—two hundred years old!—and, down the hill, there's a little stand of birches with a studio for writing. His wife's charming and was glad to meet me. If they'd been at home, I'm sure his daughters would have been charming, too. I saw photographs of them. They're both very pretty."

These daughters interested me. "What are their names, the daughters?"

My father raised his eyebrows then frowned. "Not for you," he warned. "Anyway, like I said, they weren't at home."

I imagined these pretty, nameless daughters escaping, fighting free of their charming mother and famous father. Boarding school? The L.L. Bean lake houses of friends? Paris, Florence, Rimini? Anywhere away from the big white farmhouse.

My father always returned from these long weekends exhilarated, almost starry-eyed, irrepressibly quoting the Author's apothegms which he twisted into pistols aimed at me.

Even if it was *I, Claudius* on PBS: "Too much television's just as bad as too much sugar."

When I got a mediocre grade on an Algebra test: "The difference between ignorance and stupidity is that only one is curable."

When I hesitated between mowing the lawn and clearing out the garage: "Eat the best lambchop first; better to choke on it than the bad one."

When, after a family barbecue, I repeated my cousins' criticism of their father and my uncle's of them: "Always defend the young against the old and the old against the young."

On my personal hygiene: "It's hard to be virtuous when your hair is dirty."

The year the Author won the Pulitzer Prize, my father came near acting as if *he* had. There was champagne and the promise of a racing bike. Over the celebratory supper, my father burbled with nostalgia and new anecdotes like the one about how the two of them had gotten drunk on cheap vodka, hung a speaker out the dormitory window and blasted Beethoven's *Ninth* into the quad at midnight. Another was about how the Author had been hired to write a paper for a rich but ungifted classmate who was now in the Senate.

My father chuckled at the memory of a hoax he said he and the Author had cooked up together.

"We wrote a paper proving that baseball had been invented by Edgar Allan Poe and not Abner Doubleday."

Was this my father?

In those years, he shared similar anecdotes with me at odd moments, apropos of nothing, usually when it was just the two of us in the car.

"This one weekend, we took the train to New York. Somebody's parents were away and gave us the keys to their apartment in Greenwich Village. Danish furniture, two Léger lithographs, bookcases on every wall, huge record collection. We went to a jazz club—the Village Vanguard, I think—and heard Bill Evans. We talked our way into an after-hours club and saw Lenny Bruce." While these stories were not exactly edifying, most came with a moral. "Evans and Bruce—both done in by drugs."

One Saturday, when I'd taken in the mail, I asked my father why I never saw one of the Author's letters.

"He sends them to me at work," he replied.

"Do you save them?"

"Save them? What do you think? I keep them in a special drawer. Locked," he added curtly.

All through those years and even after I went off to the same university my father attended, I was treated to the Author's advice, subjected to Authorial authority. He had a lot to say about marriage.

"Be careful not to make a girl pregnant and don't marry before thirty or after forty. Thirty-five would be ideal."

"Nature decks girls out gloriously for a decade. Remember that's to trap young men. Nature doesn't care about you or her—just wants babies."

"Adolescence is a battle between culture and hormones."

"When you're tempted to propose, ask yourself whether you'd want to talk to this person when you're both fifty."

The Author was pithy, and his maxims had scope. Some were practical; others were profound or puzzling.

"The trick is not to sell your soul, not to the Devil—and not to God, either."

"Choose your clothing carefully when you're twenty-six. It's how you'll want to dress for the rest of our life."

"Keep your overhead low, but not so low you hit your head on it."

"It's more important to choose work that makes you want to leap out of bed in the morning than a job that pays handsomely and makes you hate your alarm clock."

"A lot of risky things will seem to you like bicycle-riding: at first it seems impossible to stay up, then impossible to fall."

"Never confuse sitting still with going in every direction at once."

My father relished these philosophical nuggets, even the most cynical, praising the Author for anchoring his abstractions in his deep novelist's understanding of humanity. I wrote a lot of them down in a spiral notebook.

"An honest man admits the constancy of change; a dishonest one changes constancies."

"A potato has less potential than a farmer."

"The rich man steals; the poor man dreams of theft."

"All numbers are prices; all names are stories."

"For some people, every road is nothing but middle."

My father read all the Author's books as soon as they came out and studied the reviews, rejoicing in the good ones. The few that were bad infuriated him.

"Just listen to this moron!" he'd exclaim from his recliner then read the offending criticism aloud, scoffing after every offending sentence.

"'*This latest offering is one-fifth Graham Greene and four-fifths Mickey Spillane.*' What a hack. Even his insults are plagiarized!"

During my father's weekends in the Green Mountains, Mother was like a rubber band given a break from holding things together. Not that she was focused on me or kicked up her heels—like the rubber band, she relaxed but didn't do anything. Still, I noticed that she moved differently, took longer strides and deeper breaths, and her cooking showed more imagination. She never asked why she too wasn't invited to the Green Mountains where she could be introduced to the Author, keep company with his charming wife, and admire the pretty daughters—if they chanced to be at home. Her exclusion was simply a given. My father didn't want himself or the Author to be distracted. The male bond was exclusive, the reunion strictly stag, a duet. I can remember only one remark my mother made on the subject. I had said something about it probably being good for my father to spend a little time away from the store. Mother smiled ambiguously then, to my astonishment, she too quoted the Author, one of my father's favorite one-liners: "There's no such thing as a well-earned vacation."

The Author's books were good and most had happy endings; the kind where the camera cuts off when lovers join. Though he was deeply perceptive and free of illusions, the Author enjoyed not only a professional success but also a contented married life. If he was happy himself, why shouldn't he favor happy endings? But then why would he say things like this to my father: "Men and woman are in a perpetual war with an infinite number of truces"? I found it hard to reconcile the generous and humane novels with the moralistic strictures and scornful observations my father so loved repeating. I found none of them in the novels so they must have come from their correspondence and conversations.

After graduation, I didn't return home. I chose a booming coastal metropolis and found work that was challenging even if it didn't always make me leap out of bed every morning.

A Walgreens opened two blocks from my father's pharmacy. He lost customers and grew despondent. He became as taciturn as my mother, who by then left the house only to buy groceries. Both aged quickly as if in a race to the finish. They shed weight and appeared to me to be drying out, as if the climate in the straitened house had become parched. My visits stimulated no joy either in them or me, though I tried to cheer them up. I brought them bagels, imported cheeses, bottles of oyster sauce. I told them stories slowly and made jokes manically. I described my work and my new friends—good, talented people even if none could, I assured my father, compare to The Author. As far as I can recall, during these visits he seldom quoted the Author, but I do remember that, after dinner one night, he mentioned having gotten a letter. He pointed a finger at me and spoke solemnly, as if pronouncing a prophetic judgment. "The man's so wise. Listen to this: 'Most people live their lives in elevators—going up or down they visit the same places.'"

When customers became downright scarce, Father sold his store to a national chain of cafés and retired. He grew more querulous and withdrawn; his memory slowly dissolved like an icicle in a February thaw. Mother took care of him. He didn't thank her and she didn't complain. There was a heart attack, appointments with a cardiologist.

After his funeral, I visited Mother every other weekend. When I suggested she sell the house and move to an apartment, she said she was fine where she was, and I didn't need to worry about her, or feel I had to come so often.

On my next-to-last visit, I asked her what had become of the Author's letters.

"What letters?"

"The ones he kept at the store, in the locked drawer."

She made a sour face. "I don't know anything about that," she said.

It was a shock but not a surprise when she died eight months after my father. I was now an orphan, facing life without the parental barrier against mortality, the one you don't know is there until it's gone.

A newspaper article that said the Author was a candidate for the Nobel prize and speculated on his chances. It made me think he might not know that his old friend had died, that there were unanswered letters, and that I ought to tell him.

I had no address for the Author, not in the Green Mountains or anywhere else, so I wrote to his publisher, explaining the relationship between the Author and my late father, and asking if they would kindly forward my enclosed letter. My letter to the Author was short; each of the five drafts was briefer than the last.

A week later, I received a reply from the Author's editor. She regretted to tell me that unfortunately the Author had suffered a stroke two weeks earlier, one that was not incapacitating but which could not be called mild either. She was in touch with him, of course; they spoke regularly by phone, and she had told him about my father's death.

"He said he didn't recognize your father's name and had no recollection of him. His memory is still fairly reliable, but it's not impossible the stroke has erased your father from it. I'm terribly sorry."

Was it all true but, as the editor said, erased? Editors know all about erasures. Or was the whole business of the Author a fantasy, a self-aggrandizing delusion, an attempt to be warmed in reflected glory? Had my father and the Author even known each other? Were there no trips to Greenwich Village, Beethoven blasted out a dorm window, no weekends in the Green Mountains, no letters at all? If so, where did he go on those long weekends? Fishing trips? Another woman? Were those relentless, apodictic admonitions and chastisements, those bits of wisdom and secular proverbs, really my father's?

I don't know and I can't know.

I'm looking now at the last sentence of what will probably be the Author's final novel which, like his first, is a story of a young man freeing himself from his family and setting out on life.

The sky is a father's face; the sea a mother's breast; but all the earth is one's own.

Beezlepoint and Needleprat

1.

-Hello?

-Is this Emily Rath?

-Yes?

-The daughter of Alexander Rath?

-My God. What's happened?

-Don't be upset, Ms. Rath. Your father's fine.

-What's happened to him? Where is he?

-I'm sorry. Nothing's wrong with your father, Ms. Rath. In a sense, that's the problem.

-Who's this?

-My name is Cardew, Angela Cardew. I manage Stilton Downs Hospice here in Brewster. A short while ago your father drove into our parking lot, walked into reception, and requested to be admitted as a client. We don't say patient.

-He asked. . ?

-Mr. Rath insists he is dying and attempted to hand over both his insurance and American Express cards. He requested a room on the north side and what he called a ministering angel, preferably blonde. Ms. Rath, I can assure you we don't have walk-in trade here. He suggested that you would sign any necessary forms. But I'm sure you understand, Ms. Rath, that a doctor—

-Of course. My father, you see, you're perfectly right. I mean his health is fine. But he's been having these spells, whims really; sometimes it's his memory, just a little, you understand?

-This has happened before?

-No, no. Never. I'm completely flabbergasted. How is he? Where is he now?

-Your father is sitting just outside my office. He's well dressed, and I must say he looks in the pink. He has, however, refused to leave. Would you care to talk to him?

-Yes, yes, of course.

-Thank you. Just a minute, then.

-Emily? I heard Ms. Cardew here tell you I'm well dressed. Her office is very nice, but it's inadequately soundproofed. Incidentally, she's wearing a very becoming cream-colored sweater set, tasteful necklace, skirt about four inches below the knee. Is that correct, Ms. Cardew? Four inches? I only said that thing about a ministering angel because Ms. Cardew's given name is Angela. It says so on her desk. In brass.

-What are you doing, Daddy?

-Dying, sweetheart. Did you think it was a cry for attention? A lark?

-You're not dying.

-Oh, I'm sorry, sweetie, but we all are. I'd just like to move things along. *Der Blitz vor dem Arzten.* That's Seneca, but in German not Latin. Not yet a dead language, German, but the language of death. Do you speak German, Ms. Cardew? Or Latin? *Fulmen ante medici*? Bit of a Stoic scoundrel, Seneca, bombastic but a fair philosopher, got mixed up in politics. *Zuerst der Blitz.*

-You're not making sense.

-It's a prayer, Emily. Maybe the most sensible one of all.

-Look, you can't stay there, Daddy.

-Pity. It's a lovely place. Grounds could be out of one of your mother's favorite novels; you know, the sort that wind up with everybody happy and rich on an English estate, lots of guineas and treacle. They have green fields out here, big oaks and rolled lawns. He babbled of green fields.

-Daddy?

-You want me to go home, don't you?

-I'll come and get you.

-No. It's all right. I know when I'm not wanted. I've got my car. Henry Ford said history is more or less bunk. More or less. I memorized the speech. It's so American. This reporter asked Ford why he didn't want the country to build its defenses when Trafalgar had kept Napoleon from invading England. And Ford said, "I don't know whether Napoleon did or did not try to get across there and I don't care. It means nothing to me. History is more or less bunk. It's tradition. We don't want tradition. We want to live in the present and the only history that is worth a tinker's dam is the history we make today." Really, could anything be more American? And yet it got him in a heap of trouble. There was a libel case. World War I was going on; you'd think a guy like Henry Ford could foresee the profits to made. Hell, you'd think he'd invent the tank. But no. He refused to pay the national guardsmen. Ended by suing this reporter named McCormick for libel. This was in 1916, you understand. Verdun. The Somme. Ford won his case, and the judge awarded him—what was it?—a nickel? No, it was six cents. Exactly six cents. That was a judge with a sense of humor. More or less.

-Please put Ms. Cardew back on, Daddy.

-You want to speak to Angela? I'm warning you; the woman absolutely refuses to minister to anybody.

2.

Emily's mother did love Victorian novels which is why she named her daughters Charlotte and Emily. Her husband, an undistinguished professor of history made less ambitious by the possession of private means, was content to indulge his adored wife. In fact, he approved of everything she did with the sole exception of dying at thirty-eight. The girls went to boarding school, then college. Charlotte, the smart one, continued on to graduate school, turned down a proposal of marriage, went for her Ph.D. in American history. Emily was glad to leave school. After a summer of irresolution, she decided to train as a legal secretary. She quickly found a job, two years later married a client, the owner of three appliance stores, and quickly had a daughter of her own. Her husband objected that it was outlandish, but she called her daughter Bettina anyway, also a literary name. Four years after that, Emily's husband left her for a more easy-going woman he thought he liked better. Emily returned to work notwithstanding her divorce attorney's advice that her income would practically eliminate alimony. At this Emily smiled. Bettina developed a learning difficulty, nothing debilitating; she just mixed things up sometimes. She was laughed at in class one day when she was asked to read aloud and said *mesquite* instead of *mosquito*. It only happened with words, never numbers. Bettina was good at math, not a genius but still a natural. As for Charlotte, she preferred teaching to mothering and research to teaching. Still unwed and determined to stay that way, she landed a job with prospects on the West Coast, so the task of watching over their retired father fell on Emily. She got on better with him than did Charlotte anyway, perhaps because, unlike her sister, she was not determined to cover up his footsteps. He lived in the old house, a Victorian of course. Emily had a Cape close by and he visited almost every day, or she went to him.

Emily enjoyed her job with the lawyers, where she was the pin in the pinwheel. She also loved her daughter and father. She did not in the least resent that these three relationships formed the troika that carried her across the level steppe of her life, the triangular corral of her days. She did not long for dates or dinner parties or the life of the paired-off. Her favorite painting was *The Daughters of Edward Boit* by John Singer Sargent. None of the four Boit girls in the picture had married. She was one up on them and felt lucky that a man had entered her life, helped produce Bettina, and then had the good grace to go away.

Emily's father was turning strange, though. Long speeches poured from him unseasonably, punctuated by random bits of recollected erudition, like Seneca's prayer or Ford's libel suit. He was likely to say anything, even to Bettina, though he always made a kind of inappropriate sense. The world could be his class or his confessor. Bettina and he doted on each other. Emily was always moved when she watched them together. Her father perplexed and troubled Emily; every day he seemed more loving and wearier of life. The lightning before the doctors.

3.

The two of them were in the little garden behind the house. Bettina had taken her grandfather Alexander by the hand and made him name all the plants. Emily, making dinner in the kitchen, watched them from the window over the sink. Her father was talking, and she leaned into the window to hear better. He had explained fascination to her one night when she was little and couldn't sleep because of a horror movie. He said that fascination is feeling attraction and repulsion at the same time. Now he was telling Bettina not about the plants but about when he was young.

-When I was a youngster, I looked up the definition of the word *weed.* My mother always complained about the weeds in her garden, you see. Do you know what a weed is exactly, my dear? Well, according to the dictionary a weed is any plant growing where you don't want it to. Wild roses could be weeds if what you want is, say, a hosta like this or a Siberian iris like that over there. A blood orchid could be a weed if what you had in mind is just a common begonia. I was shocked by the subjectivity, the downright relativism of the idea that the identity of an actual physical object—an almost unlimited number of them, in fact—depended entirely on mutable opinion. Something could be a weed to one person and not to another, or even to the same person if his opinion changed after lunch or if he was in another part of the garden. Weed, not-weed. A few inches and a caprice could make the difference. Well, dear, I was only six or seven, but I felt the despair of radical relativism, the acidie of the Hellenistic Skeptic. I thought, what if history's just the gossip and rumors enough people happen to believe, or are convinced to believe? What if the past is water? No wonder we deny freedom to our ancestors when they're completely in our hands. The dead are robbed of every right, including that of defending themselves. Well, as you can imagine, all this made me despondent. It was as if in a moment the world had sublimated, turned to vapor. Do you know what I did then? Well, I went back to the dictionary. You can't doubt the dictionary, can you? I looked up this plant. It's called veronica, also known as speedwell. I looked up toadflax. We had lots of toadflax and Mother hated it. Well, these definitions could not have been more precise or absolute. Now I had to ask myself what this meant. A general term like "weed" is really shorthand for "I don't like this here." Specific terms are different; it doesn't take a horticulturist to tell veronica from toadflax. So, is truth just a believed illusion or is it objective, the same for everybody? Might history be reliable if you look hard enough and put your opinions aside? Yet if you *do* ignore your opinions what you get isn't history at all but a chronicle. You get this and this *followed by* that, not this *because of* that, if you see what I mean. *Because of.* That's the sound of a door opening on meaning but also the lack of meaning. *Because of's* a door that swings both in and out. So where was I? I haven't any wish to be the historian of my life. How can people write memoirs and not die of shame?

Bettina stood still and listened to all this calmly, let it wash over her, but looked serious, as if she understood. Maybe she does understand, thought Emily, just not the words.

4.

Emily had the habit of rubbing her right index finger against fabrics like the edging of blankets, jeans pockets, lace, upholstery. Depending on the surface, she used her nail, her cuticle, or the side of her digit. The rubbing was semi-conscious. Something about the resistance, the smoothness and sound comforted her, lowered her blood pressure, slowed her breathing. She'd always believed this habit, which she did her best to hide, originated in her unremembered infancy when she must have done it to soothe herself. So, Emily was surprised when her daughter began doing it too. Bettina, however, fixed the rubbing on a single object, a cosmetic bag she found in her mother's bureau. Emily would have liked to wean Bettina away from the bag, and made some half-hearted efforts to do so, but she felt hypocritical. After all, Bettina had watched her in moments of stress rubbing her slacks, the couch, her shirt collar. Could such a trait be inherited?

Bettina had her little sport bag under the covers. Emily knew it was there but pretended not to. Her daughter's school day had not gone well. She had said *scandals* instead of *sandals*, and there had been laughter but even Bettina admitted it was funny to picture Roman legions marching all over the Empire in their scandals. In fact, Bettina was becoming resigned to this sort of contretemps; she no longer felt humiliated and took her mix-ups philosophically. It only happens *some*times, she had said pensively when telling her mother about it. She didn't cry at all, though Emily suspected that was because she'd done so already.

Bettina's grandfather had his own way of encouraging her. He compiled a list of accomplished dyslexics and told alarming jokes, such as one about a boy who advised his girlfriend he'd pick her up "somewhere between eight and seven." Alexander never mentioned Mrs. Malaprop but he did take to imitating her, not in mockery but solidarity. At dinner one night he said, "Please pass the harassment" instead of "asparagus." At McDonald's he'd ordered "fried Frenchies" instead of "French fries," which just broke Bettina up. The school did as well as it could. Bettina had all the accommodations the law prescribed and a sympathetic fourth-grade teacher.

Bedtime. Emily was about to resume her reading of *The Wind in the Willows*, more a favorite of hers than of Bettina's. Toad and his fads, stolid Badger, innocent Mole, dashing Ratty—this green, watery world was exotic to Bettina but familiar to her mother, reared on *Now We Are Six*, *Through the Looking Glass*, and *Water Babies*. Emily drew her breath and made ready to wax pantheistic over the poetical chapter titled "The Piper at the Gates of Dawn" when Bettina stopped her.

-Do you know why I sometimes mix words up, Mommy? It's because of Mrs. Beezlepoint and Mr. Needleprat. They get cross with each other and then they make mistakes.

-Oh, and who are Mrs. Beezlepoint and Mr. Needleprat?

-The librarians in my brain, of course. We all have librarians up there.

Where did this come from, Emily wondered. Then she remembered that her father had taken Bettina into Boston for the day. They went to the Aquarium, looked into Faneuil Hall, ate pizza and ice cream in Quincy Market, stopped by a toy store. But what impressed the child most was the Boston Public Library. Alexander had arranged for them to look over the special collections but what stuck with Bettina were the mechanics of the place—the request forms and retrievals, the banks of computers, the hush of hundreds of people. Librarians she now conceived as lordly creatures, supercilious angels. This romantic recollection, Emily guessed, gave birth to the touchy Mrs. Beezlepoint and the irritable Mr. Needleprat.

-Mostly they get along. When I have to think of something, they go and get the right words out of the stacks. It's when they're arguing that they pull out the wrong ones.

Emily thought of how, despite her precautions, Bettina would have overheard her and her ex-husband going at it. She had learned that her daughter liked to find out about the world by a sort of experimental mythologizing rather than by simply asking. Bettina was trying her hand at brain science.

-Mr. Needleprat wears suspenders and a vest and a bow tie and serious brown shoes. Mrs. Beezlepoint likes maroon and purple dresses. She never wears suits. They're both old and have to wear glasses. They each have a little bedroom which is where they go when I go to sleep, but they're always on call in case I have like a dream, so they have to get up a lot at night. Like Grampa. It makes them cranky.

Emily hesitated. Bettina didn't really need the difference between fantasy and reality pointed out to her.

-What do they fight over?

-All sorts of things. I don't always know. Sometimes it's politics or movies. Stuff like that. Mrs. Beezlepoint is in charge of all the words starting from A to M and Mr. Needleprat from N to Z. But sometimes, just to spite each other, they'll—what's the word?

-Does it come before or after M?

-*After*, I think. Like an egg? Like, like pooch?

-Poach?

-Yes. They *poach*. Grampa told me that poaching's wrong but not as wrong as stealing, but I really couldn't see the difference and Grampa said it was a—a delicatessen distinction.

-Yes, dear. It is. Delicate.

-So, if Mrs. Beezlepoint and Mr. Needleprat can patch things up, if they can cooperate, if they could just tell each other that they really, really like each other, and not poach or tease, I wouldn't get mixed up.

-And if they got more *sleep*?

- I get it, Mommy. Okay. Let's hear what stupid thing Toad's doing now.

Emily could see the finger moving faintly under the blanket, like a bird's heartbeat.

5.

Charlotte had splendid news. She toned down her exuberance with Emily, relying on her little sister to provide the re-inflation. Charlotte wondered if by any chance their father might be there. This was disingenuous; it was Friday night just before dinnertime. She knew Alexander would be there. To him, she crowed, of course. She couldn't help it.

Charlotte's dissertation on Theodore Roosevelt and Mark Twain had been accepted by Oxford University Press. At the very least, it meant a tenure review, perhaps celebrity. The press's reviewers had gushed. Alexander Rath had never published a book, only a few obscure essays which he was pleased to dismiss as his "indefinite articles." As always, he was hurt by Charlotte's need to compete with him, at this odd buckling of a daughter's love, yet he was also pleased, proud and, to her, gracious. As they sat down to enjoy roast capon, he explained to Bettina that her Aunt Charlotte was going to be the author of a book, a fat one, too. Bettina wanted to know if it would be in the library, the big one in the city.

-We'll get our very own copy, said Emily.

Bettina was disappointed.

-Then it *won't* be in the library?

-Of course, it will. We can go visit it in the library after it gets published.

-It's going to be punished?

-No, sweetie, *published.* That means when it's printed and goes on sale and people can buy it.

It was two weeks later that Emily pulled off her great coup at work. Was she inspired by her sister's success or were the heavens aligned to favor *les filles* Rath?

The story was full of complications, not all of them legal, and Emily knew she would have to simplify it to tell the tale. She gave it a private title: "How I May Have Saved A Semi-Innocent Man." The firm had been tied up for months with the case. The client was their biggest, a former CEO charged with what Emily, for the sake of clarity, decided to call embezzlement which sounded to Bettina like Beezlepoint.

Huge sums of company money had been diverted to an account on a Caribbean island, books cooked. The prosecutors immunized the former auditor and CFO who then damned the client in open court. The client was baffled. Sure, he'd cut some corners, who didn't, but nothing like this, nothing so unambiguously outside the law. They're lying, he insisted, bitter and bewildered. The prosecution was able to find out that there was indeed a Caribbean account in his name, though the tropical bankers drew the line at disclosing any details. Their business, after all, was secrecy. The client was convicted. Of course, he would appeal but on what grounds? Procedural? Substantive? Emily had been in court three times. She listened less than she looked and what she scrutinized were the government's witnesses. The librarians in her own brain got busy and pulled out a hunch. She conducted a little social research, made a few calls. All this she did on her own, which was perhaps improper, but she uncovered a key fact: the auditor's first wife's sister was the CFO's first cousin. She convinced her bosses to find a way to get more information out of the Caribbean bank the old-fashioned way, with a bribe. There were two more accounts in the same bank, one in the name of the CFO, the other in the auditor's. With the aid of a confederate at the bank, they had arranged for the funds to be transferred into these accounts within weeks of the verdict. The conviction made them overconfident; being greedy, they were also impatient. The devious plot all came out like meat expertly extracted from a lobster claw.

There was a celebratory party at Legal Sea Foods thrown by the CEO who offered Emily her choice of his first-born or a Lexus and, after three Laphroaigs, suggested he would be willing to divorce his second wife and make her his third. Emily just smiled tightly. However, she did find it possible to accept a hefty bonus.

Alexander loved her story. Bettina loved her new dollhouse—a big, gingerbread Victorian like Grampa's but, as he observed, cheaper to heat.

After Bettina had been bathed and put to bed, Alexander said he was ready to go home but stayed seated on the sofa. He patted the cushion and Emily sat down next to him, surprised when he put his arm around her.

-I suppose you know how pleased I am with you, Emily, and not just over this clever coup at work. But I wonder if you can imagine how proud your mother would be, how she'd just eat Bettina up, and how I feel knowing she can't. I used to think feelings weren't much good for anything. I expect you and your sister noticed this. I was stuck in the time before machines took over, when people thought reason made us human; now it's our feelings. The truth is this isthmus we're on is where the baboon greets the PC. All the mammals are able to feel shame, fear, even sympathy, and it's out of these feelings that we made ourselves so complicated, social, and sometimes moral, once in a while even noble. Nobility isn't happiness but a good way of not being happy. Nobility lies in not giving in to feelings but there's no nobility if they aren't there. I'm talking about the feelings those crooks didn't have. They're all right here, incidentally, in the prefrontal lobe. Right here.

Alexander pointed to his forehead exactly as Bettina had done when telling her mother about Beezlepoint and Needleprat.

-It's the last part of the brain to develop, except maybe for Bettina. People with damage in that region can be sociopaths. They don't connect the pain of punishment with the action that merited it, or the reward of pleasure with doing the decent thing. Rules are lost on them. They're not masters beyond good and evil but dangerous worms. They never feel the tickle of meaninglessness, have neither empathy nor suicidal tendencies. They ain't got no angst at all. If we hadn't evolved this lobe and its tangled *Menschlichkeit*, we'd have destroyed ourselves by now. One of Epicurus's arguments that the gods don't pay attention to our prayers is that we aren't all dead. Nietzsche said the thought of suicide got him through many a bad night. Reason on its own would have done us in, according to Rousseau. But Shaw put it best: after the age of three none of us manage our affairs as well as a tree does. It wasn't their stealing that was so wicked, was it? It was the framing their boss. Look, I know how it upsets you that Bettina makes these little mistakes with words, but I've never seen her make one with her feelings. Listen to me. I know more than I used to. I'm dying but my brain is in denial. When I go, you'll have money. You can ask me for as much as you like, of course. I'd give it all to you now, but I think of Lear. His big goof wasn't giving away his kingdom, or even dividing it up, but doing it before he died—and having two daughters deficient in the prefrontal lobe department.

-You think Charlotte and I—?

-That came out badly. Don't get me wrong. You're a pair of Cordelias.

-Then?

-What I mean is men aren't all forked worms or inefficient trees and life isn't all duty either. What I mean is, don't you think it might be time to have a man in your life—or, if you prefer, a woman?

-Daddy!

-I don't know everything. Okay, I'll just look in on Bettina and then I'll go. Thanks for indulging me while I wallow.

-Daddy?

-Yes?

-Do *you* have bad nights when you think about suicide?

-Shh.

6.

On Harry Hojny's first day in his new school he got into a fight or rather he was attacked. After lunch, two boys cornered the new kid in an alcove. The pair were not so much bullies as badly reared xenophobes and Harry had an accent. True, it was about as faint as the aroma of honeysuckle in August, but there it was. They began by shoving him into an alcove, then came the name-calling followed shortly by fists. Harry put up a stout defense considering he was outnumbered, outweighed, and had his back against the wall. He caught one of the boys right on the nose. Enraged by the blood the boy butted Harry in the stomach but then, cunningly, pulled away and grabbed his friend. "You're my witness," he hissed, spreading the blood all over his face. They headed for the principal's office.

All this Bettina observed from across the corridor, crouching behind the water fountain, too shocked to intervene. Neither Mrs. Beezlepoint nor Mr. Needleprat could retrieve a single word. The bell rang. Harry wiped his face and returned to class, Bettina following.

Half an hour later a messenger showed up in the classroom. Harry was summoned to the principal's office. Bettina begged her teacher to let her go too but the teacher said no, of course not. Harry glanced at her suspiciously.

He was back in ten minutes looking impassive and took his seat. Bettina managed to pass him a short note. "I saw." Harry read it, crumpled it up, and didn't look at her. Bettina wrote a second, even briefer note. "Detention?" Harry gave the smallest nod that could be called a nod.

The moment school was over Bettina borrowed Marcia's cell phone and called her grandfather, who was to pick her up. Luckily, he hadn't left yet.

-I'll be late, Grampa. I have something I have to do at school. Tell Mommy.

-When should I come for you?

-Come at four o'clock.

-Are you okay, sweetheart?

-I'm fine. Just going to be a little late. *Okay*?

Alexander didn't ask further questions. He respected that level of impatience.

Bettina went to the library which served as the detention hall. When the teacher in charge objected that her name wasn't on the list, Bettina said she wanted to use the library, grabbed a book, and sat down next to Harry.

Harry's father arrived minutes later. Adam Hojny was a tall man. He wore jeans with suspenders and a flannel shirt. Bettina tried hard to read his face, to tell if he was angry or stressed or exasperated or what. Adam talked first to the teacher, then motioned for Harry to join him at the side of the room. Bettina strained to listen. Adam's accent was much heavier than his son's. He told Harry the principal had called him, that he'd had to leave work. How could he bloody a classmate's nose on his first day? Harry looked at the floor.

Bettina got up, went over to them, pulled Adam by the sleeve, and told him what she had seen and that it wasn't Harry's fault *at all.*

Harry refused to look at her. He wasn't afraid of his father or grateful to her. He just looked disgusted.

In the car, Bettina told her grandfather the whole story of Harry Hojny. He could hardly help being reminded of what Emily had done for the CEO, this common sympathy with the unjustly accused and the willingness to do something about it. Bettina said she liked Harry, but he didn't like anybody. Well, he *did* talk to her a little during detention, after his father left, though he didn't say much.

-What did he say?

-That his mother's dead and that he hates our school.

-It isn't surprising, given his welcome. They just moved?

-I guess.

-What about his father?

-What?

-Did you like Mr. Hojny too?

-He was okay, I guess. I mean he didn't yell at Harry or anything, and he listened to me. Actually, he thanked me. Harry said his dad's a carpenter. Why are carpenters called carpenters when they don't work on carpets?

-You're right. It comes from an old word for wagon, actually. Carpenters used to make wagons.

-Little red wagons?

-No, big wooden ones.

-That's silly.

-All words are stories, sweetie, and sometimes the stories are old. Hojny's a Polish name, I think. I wonder what it means.

-Harry said his father designs sets too. What's that?

-It means he makes the scenery for plays.

-Like on the stage?

-Yes.

-Then maybe Hojny means set designer in Polish. Anyway, Harry left Poland with his mother and father when he was six. His father got a job and then Harry's mother died and then his father got another job and they moved and now he has to go to a school where boys hit him, and the principal puts him in retention for no reason at all. It's not fair.

-And yet he's already made one new friend.

-Who?

-You know perfectly well. And it's *de*tention, though *re*tention makes much more sense. You have to wonder what a principal thinks of her school when she punishes you by keeping you there even longer.

Alexander dropped Bettina off and drove home. He called Information and got the listing for Hojny. There was only one and it was new. After dinner he phoned, explained who he was, welcomed Adam to town as grandly as if he were the mayor, and listened contentedly to some charmingly accented praise for his granddaughter.

-Where were you born, Adam?

-Krakow. I am now citizen here. I do woodwork, cabinet-making, furniture, sometimes framing. And sets for theater. Doesn't pay much but is work of love. Harry is also work of love, you know. He is good boy, but he has no mother and now he has had to move and is lonely.

-Adam, Adam. Were you named after the great Adam Mickiewicz?

-You know Mickiewicz, Mr. Rath?

-Of course. Born in Lithuania but Polish through and through. *Pan Tadeusz*, *Crimean Sonnets*, *Conrad Wollenrod*. I believe he's buried in your hometown with the kings, so I figured.

-Wonderful you know Mickiewicz.

-My granddaughter's named for Catherine Ludovica Magdalena Bettina Brentano von Arnim, a contemporary of your Mickiewicz, by the way. They could have met. Goethe might have had them both over to dinner at Weimar. Say, that gives me an idea, Adam. Would you and Harry come and have dinner with *me*?

-Dinner?

-Yes. Let's say Saturday, if it's convenient. No need to dress up. Nothing fancy. I'll make a roast. Very easy.

-Well. . . if you like. Very kind. Yes. It would be an honor, Mr. Rath.

-Excellent. Six o'clock, then? Here's my address.

7.

Alexander was feeling expansive and devilish. It was exhilarating to be a host again. Bettina had persuaded Harry to explore the house's upstairs with its oddities and heirlooms, including an ancient wind-up phonograph which played a wondrous, unintelligible disk called *Cohn on the Telephone*. Emily was looking very nice indeed and, despite being told it was unnecessary, Adam had dressed up. Toward Emily he was courtly without being stiff. She exerted herself to make conversation; after all, she and Adam had plenty to talk about: the school, their children, the detention story, the best bakery in town, the best shoe store, the theater, Krakow. If all this should prove insufficient, if there should be a hiatus, there was the food and whatever screed might come out of Alexander's mouth. Her father's speeches made Emily apprehensive less for their recondite content than their timing. There was that weird business with the hospice, too. Her father was becoming more unpredictable, and she worried about dementia, depression, about his driving Bettina to and from school.

Bettina was crazy about the idea of the dinner, but Emily had dreaded it. Nevertheless, before she knew it, she was enjoying herself. Adam knew a lot about the theater, which interested her; he had acted in his youth and even confessed to writing a couple of bad plays. He summarized the plot of one, a comedy in which a Pole is mistaken for a Russian and vice versa.

Meanwhile, Harry took to Alexander who seemed to know just how to talk to him. The boy loosened up. Over the roast beef and potatoes Alexander asked him what he was most interested in.

Harry answered at once. *Science.*

-Harry likes astronomy, paleontology, physics, said Adam. Harry is very serious boy, much more than me. He will be engineer, I think.

-And he has a good uppercut, evidently. Do you know what the Industrial Revolution is, Harry?

-Factories.

-Yes. The application of science to the means of production. Science gave us the Enlightenment which was, on the whole, a good thing.

-It gave us democracy, said Adam. It displaced the Church, even, now, in Poland.

-It's no less true to say that democracy gave us science.

-How do you mean, Mr. Rath?

-Call me Alexander, please.

-Daddy!

-Harry, you want to be a scientist, an engineer perhaps? I'm going to tell you why the Industrial Revolution began in England. It's an instructive story, with a moral. Know what a moral is?

-The boring bit at the end of a story.

-This is a clever boy, Bettina. You should always sit beside him.

-Are you clover, Harry?

-Clover?

-Clever.

-I want to be. Why'd you say clover?

-Sometimes Bettina mixes up her words, Harry, said Emily, looking pained, but Bettina was unembarrassed and eager to explain.

-I have these two librarians in my head, Harry, and—

-Tell Harry about it later, dear. Grampa wants to talk.

-Mrs. Beezlepoint goofed, Bettina whispered to Harry.

-Very well, said Alexander. England and the Industrial Revolution. Up to the sixteenth century the English economy ran on wood, like everybody else's. By the end of that century, though, they had pretty much used up all their forests. They'd hit what economists call a *wall*. In the past, societies that used up their forests declined. For example, Mesopotamia fell victim to deforestation and the same thing happened to Venice, which cut down all its trees to make ships. So, running out of forests, in the early sixteen hundreds the English passed a law forbidding the burning of wood. The economy now had to run on coal, which

England had plenty of. But there was a problem. Coal had to be mined and the mines flooded and needed pumping out. In those days this was done by horsepower. The horses would be hitched to a wheel and the wheel to ropes that would pull up buckets. The problem was that, as the mines went deeper and deeper, more and more horses had to be added to pull more water and these horses needed more and more oats. Before long the horses were eating so many oats that the oats exceeded the value of the coal. You can see the problem. Now what saved England, and made her the first industrial society, was the democratization of science. In those days scientists were novelties. The universities turned out quite a lot of them but only a lucky few were hired to ornament the estates of the aristocracy. They would do after-dinner tricks for the guests. You know the sort of thing—booms and flashes. The point is that the supply of scientists in England exceeded the demands of the gentry. What were these hungry surplus scientists to do? Well, what they *did* was offer lectures to the paying public. Now, what happened next is rather interesting, Harry, one of those little accidents on which empires turn. A certain ironmonger in Western England bought a ticket to one such lecture where a scientist did some tricks with vacuums. The ironmonger, who hadn't been to college like the scientist, had a brainstorm. He pictured how a vacuum could be used to operate a piston and how this piston could be made into an efficient pump. The vacuum pump uses physical principles to push water up and has a huge mechanical advantage over anything horses can accomplish. So, the Industrial Revolution started in England because a smart ironmonger heard an unemployed scientist.

-That's fascinating, Adam declared.

-I think I get it, said Harry uncertainly.

-Can we *please* be excused, asked Bettina impatiently.

-Let's go into the living room, Emily suggested diplomatically.

8.

July the Fourth. Independence demands collective celebration. It was a pretty day. Henry James said the two loveliest English words are *summer afternoon.* On the lawn, Bettina was teaching Harry to play croquet. In the kitchen, Adam was showing Emily how to make pirogi. Why not also celebrate the independence Mickiewicz and Chopin dreamed of, both dying romantically in exile?

Alexander Rath sits in the shade of his wide porch watching the children in the sun, listening to the noises from the kitchen. He is feeling particularly well. His bones, nerves, and alimentary canal are not a bit cross with him today. At noon, Charlotte phoned, only nine o'clock for her. His elder daughter had sounded like somebody else, someone simpler and happier. She spoke in an unfamiliar, bubbly soprano rather than her customary grave alto.

-I'm getting married! I know, I know. It's awfully sudden but we're sure so why wait? Mark's a microbiologist. He was born in Taiwan and grew up in Oakland. Mark's his American name. In Chinese he's Hsi-Wei. He's brilliant and beautiful and sweet and he has the good taste to love my book and, of course, we'll *always* love each other exactly the way we do now. We both want Bettina to have a cousin and we both want a house, everything normal and clean and boring, only it isn't boring at all. Now listen. All three of you are going to come out here for the wedding. No arguments, Dad. Just get used to the idea. It's next month, so Bettina won't miss even one day of school.

Alexander thinks. Would they be happy all the time, ever after? Would it be another edition of Mrs. Beezlepoint and Mr. Needleprat, with the spats and snits yet to come? It's discreet to cut the camera when happiness is still the ending, when we know the family will survive, when life has gotten its way. Genes from all over. Rather splendid to have a Chinese son-in-law—maybe also a Pole. Who knows? Toss all the DNA into the majestic Melting Pot.

He muses on the brain. The human brain is the glory and scourge of the planet: it makes us independent of nature and so responsible for it. There's no responsibility without freedom. Freedom is the unreckonable variation of possibility. Trillions of cells and synapses and worlds within worlds linking and zapping and secreting. Bettina's confusions are endearing but the fact is we are all confused; all our paths are strewn with banana peels.

-No, no! Not under the shed! cries Bettina. Harry is ruthless with his mallet but wants her approval.

-Did I do it right?

Agreeable badinage wafts from the kitchen.

-Dumpling is a funny word.

-So's pirogi. Is *one* called a piroga or a pirog?

-A pirogue is boat in Louisiana. Men from Texas like it if you call them Tex, but the ones from Louisiana don't like if you call them Louise.

-You're beginning to sound like my father.

-Thank you.

Alexander continued his disorderly musing. He recalled a young secretary in the English department the men had nicknamed Easeful Death because we were all half in love with her. She married out of academia and moved on. A wise woman.

It's feels wrong to live longer than your father. What would one say to him?

This is her house; it's her. Big and Victorian like those complicated books with the dénouements she so enjoyed, the sudden fortune from Australia, the misplaced children miraculously found, the lovers tidily coupled. Will they sell the place? Of course they will, why not?

Alexander recollects the light verse he'd written the previous night with his old Pelikan, his link to tradition. Wherever had the impulse come from? Some spontaneous overflow of emotion? Despair that seeks comfort in gnomic rhymes? What was it about, or any poem, but still being alive? Even if he could somehow emend the thing, it still wouldn't be worthy to kiss the toenails of a Crimean sonnet.

Alexander strode into the kitchen, all smiles, kissed Emily on the cheek, grinned at Adam, patted his shoulder, then went upstairs. If he had a gun, he could do it now. Sitting down at his desk, he opened a blue folder:

As days dawdle and years bolt by
it seems more suitable to die
than play at the immortal sage
doling green wisdom in gray age.
The playwright nods but keeps writing
small talk, monologues, inditing
barren affinities, routine:
on his static set a changeless scene.
Like parched twigs, bones grow brittle,
prostates large, libidos little.
In the end, finales dictate
the burden of the actors' fate.
Tragedies spell a family's doom;
comedies end in the bedroom.

Petite Suite de Renommage

1. L'Immigré Ambitieux – Humoresque Hébraïque en sol-majeur pour Clarinette, Cornemuse, et Tambour

When my mother boasted to my grandfather that I had gotten an A on a paper about *The Great Gatsby* for high school English, he asked to see it. I would have preferred my mother not to have bragged and my grandfather not to have asked. Unlike his daughter's, Granddad's love was less than unconditional.

My grandfather was a wry, reluctant-to-retire professor, who I figured for a tough grader. He was also Jewish. I once heard somebody ask if he was observant and I remember his answer was "from a safe distance." Like most kids, where religion was concerned, I went with my nuclear family. Mom had as much faith as an ear of corn, an atheist of the indifferent rather than militant sort. Rumor had it that my dad was raised Episcopalian, but he never mentioned it. He was laconic generally. On the other hand, my grandfather the professor would talk about anything. I thought of him when I came across Ezra Pound's otherwise poor definition of a professor as "a man who has to talk for an hour."

When we went to his house for Sunday dinner, Granddad said my essay was all right, maybe a little wordy. Then the questioning began. Had I considered making especially long sentences into two sentences? I said I'd do just that next time. He asked if I were familiar with the device of the involved narrator. I admitted I wasn't but knew he was referring to Nick Carraway. Did I like the idea of reinventing oneself, the way Jim Gatz made himself into Jay Gatsby? I was growing impatient and said I wasn't sure. The interrogation went on. Next, he wanted to know what I thought of Meyer Wolfsheim, a character whom I didn't mention in the paper or think about while writing it. I said I thought

Wolfsheim was just some big crook Gatsby was tangled up with. When he recommended two books about Fitzgerald, I thought he was finished, but he was in an expansive mood and said he wanted to tell me a story. Grandfather always had a story. His lectures must have been peppered with for instances. I suppose that, if you paid attention, you could learn a lot from his anecdotes; but, when I was little, I thought his stories boring. I just wanted to go outside, find some other kids, and play.

In the years before I hit puberty and discovered consciousness, I lived the life of a healthy animal. History was a mirage of shadowy presidents and spectral generals, the future simply a blank. There was only the present. I didn't know I'd die or that the past was full of people like me—many of them far better than me. I hadn't heard Bach or read Plato, let alone Scott Fitzgerald. What I knew about America was that it led the Free World and that I had to pledge allegiance to it every morning before the bible reading. The reading was always from the New Testament. I didn't know what a testament was or that there were two of them. I could do my times tables, knew how to ride a bike, the rules of baseball, that cowboys never had to brush their teeth, go to the bathroom, or change clothes. But by the time I got to eleventh grade, I still didn't know much, but I was a decidedly less healthy animal.

After dinner, my grandfather had invited me into his wood-paneled, book-crammed study. He seated himself behind his desk in the big leather chair that I used to think of, with a little shudder, as his throne. I sat on the other side of the desk in the hard black chair with the name and seal of his university on it. I felt like one of his students.

"It's an American story," he began, "with a twist, a bit like *Gatsby*, except it ends in a laugh instead of a murder."

"A funny story?" I said to assert myself a little.

He surprised me with another question, an unexpected non-sequitur.

"Do you know when Jews became white?"

"What?"

About three-quarters of my grandfather's questions were rhetorical. Like Socrates, he answered most of them himself.

"Not until after Israel won the Six-Day War."

"Uh-huh."

"Bear that in mind," he cautioned and pushed himself back from the desk, stretched out his legs. "In America, what year it is matters less than what generation you are. This story goes back about seventy years. It's about an enterprising fellow named Solomon Feigenbaum. First generation. Sol got some capital together and started a business on the Bowery making low-end women's dresses and what were called housecoats. He began with just half a dozen local women and four Singer machines. But he prospered and expanded. Sol treated his staff so well that they wouldn't unionize, even when he told them they should, that it was fine by him. Sol was thriving. Got married, had kids, moved uptown to a nice apartment, but he wasn't content. He had money but he yearned for acceptance. He wanted to be in the club and he aimed high—not just the Rotary or the Optimists. He wanted to join the Chamber of Commerce. But the problem was he had a disqualifying name.

"Sol Feigenbaum wasn't a bad Jew, just not an enthusiastic one. He paid his dues to the synagogue so he could take his family to high holiday services. He lit Yahrzeit candles when he remembered and gave his employees bonuses for Chanukah. But he hated his name.

"Well, when a lawyer friend told Sol that all he had to do to change his name was go to City Hall, fill out a form, and pay a hundred dollars. Sol was excited. But he was clever, a man with foresight, a man with a plan.

"He went to Probate Court, filled in the form, handed over the hundred, and changed his name. Officially, he became Francis X. Kelly."

"Why Kelly?" I asked. "I mean, if he was aiming for the top, why something Irish?"

Grandfather held up a professorial finger. "The Irish became white long before 1967."

"Yeah, but still."

The finger came up again accompanied this time with a sly grin. "Patience."

"Okay."

"Two weeks later, Sol, who was now Frank Kelly, went *back* to Probate Court, filled in another form, and gave the city another hundred bucks. This time he changed his name to J. Porter Doubleday. The J was for Jefferson."

"So, he thought better of Kelly?"

Grandfather shook his head. "Man with a plan."

"What plan?"

"Patience, remember?"

"Okay."

"Sol wangled an invitation to a reception at the Chamber of Commerce. It was a kind of recruiting session for potential members, successful businessmen. The members all wore three-piece tailored suits and nametags. They circulated among the candidates. One of them came up to Sol, a tall fellow who looked like he had grown up with a twin named trust fund. Sol stood about five-four. Old Money looked scornfully down on the short parvenu and asked what his business was. Sol told him. Now, Sol Feigenbaum had an accent that he couldn't get rid of in Probate Court. Mr. Establishment smirked and asked Sol's name. Sol answered proudly. Doubleday, J. Burton Doubleday. The man scoffed, laughed. 'Oh, come now. And what was it *before* it was

Doubleday?' 'Ah, you found me out,' Sol confessed with an apologetic little Yiddish shrug. 'It was Kelly.'"

2. *Je Suis Spartacus – Menuet pour Ford Coupé et Orchestre à Cordes Déguisé en sol majeur*

I was born in 1942 in Calhoun, Iowa. I can't claim I grew up in Iowa, only that I got bigger, older, and increasingly keen to be somewhere else. Like Calhoun the politician, Calhoun the town couldn't be called progressive; it was the sort of place where everybody needs to know which church you go to. I'm the only child my parents had time to have. They named me Harvey, Harvey Stump. My father was drafted two months after I was born and killed in the Port Chicago explosion two years later along with 319 others. When I first found out about my father's death, I thought he was blown up in Illinois and wondered why the Navy would be loading explosives on a ship in the middle of the country. Later, I found out that Port Chicago was thirty-five miles north of San Francisco, not a port at all but a munitions depot.

Another thing I asked my mother about was how she and my father had wound up in Calhoun. "We was just driving west," she said, "and the Ford broke down here, so here we stayed."

The rented house that my classmates called a shack was on the edge of town, with farmland out back that stretched all the way to the North Pole, for all I knew. The house was very small, just four rooms, but neat which didn't stop my classmates from calling it a shack, Stump's shack. Mom supported us by working as a cook and dishwasher in Calhoun's single eatery. Mr. Papadakis called it the Omega Diner. The Omega—maybe his car broke down too. I liked the diner; it was the authentic kind, a refitted silver railroad car. I liked the smells from the deep fryer and the red cooler by the door with soft drink bottles floating in melting ice. Papadakis didn't pay my mother much, but he was fat and friendly. A couple times when I was running a fever and couldn't go to school Mom took me to the diner for the day. Papadakis gave me a grilled cheese and cherry Coke on the house. He and the Omega were all right, but I didn't like my teachers, my classmates, the pinched disapproving faces of the grown-ups, or the jokes about my last name. I didn't care for the flatness of the prairie either. Iowa's low, undulating hills just made the flatness feel more relentless. In general, I wasn't content with the Hawkeye State. It wasn't only that I didn't fit in but that I didn't belong. I dreamed of picking up the journey my parents were on when the Ford broke down. I resented my father for getting blown up, my mother for working so many hours. I was aggrieved with both and especially for the name with which they saddled me but especially for stopping in Calhoun. How hard could it have been to get a new drive belt, a set of spark plugs, a new drive shaft? I felt they broke down like the Ford, settling for just where they happened to be.

I was twelve when my mother got sick. It turned out to be cancer, diagnosed too late. She wrote a letter to May, her sister in California. I hadn't known that I had an aunt who hadn't stopped in Iowa. Apparently, May and Mom had this big fight. Mom wouldn't say what it was about, but I think it was about my father. Anyway, May had written a couple of letters to mother with a return address on them, a return address to conjure with: North Hollywood, California. When Mom couldn't work anymore and I couldn't take care of her properly, May drove all the way to Calhoun to be with her. She looked like my mother but slimmer, younger, and healthier. There was a lot of crying and hugging and when my mother died a week later, we buried her and then, like my father, I was shipped off to California. I had to hide how happy I was about it. I almost cheered as we headed west out of town. Except for when I thought of my mother and got weepy, the road trip was wonderful.

Aunt May never married. She lived in a little bungalow that was painted blue with pink trim and worked in the commissary at Republic

Studios on Radford Avenue. May liked her fun. She went out with a lot of men, drank, came home late. But with me she was pretty strict, making sure I did my homework, went to bed at a decent hour, and stayed clean. But she let me watch a lot of TV and bought me new clothes then a second-hand bike. Some nights she let me cook us hot dogs and hamburgers on a grill. I liked my new school and made some friends. But even they called me Stump, just like the kids in Calhoun.

When I graduated from high school, Aunt May said and I agreed it was time for me to get a proper job. When I said I wanted to work in pictures, like her, she said, "I don't work in pictures, Harvey. I work in the commissary." I thought that working in a studio commissary in North Hollywood was much cooler than working in a diner in Calhoun but didn't say so. I did say, "But here I am—in *Hollywood*!" May made a noise and a face. "*North* Hollywood."

I'll skip over the nothing jobs and get to the one that thrilled me. Aunt May heard about a call for extras on one of those costume epics that were popular at the time, Hollywood reimagining Antiquity with a soundtrack. I'd never heard of the company making the film, Bryna Productions, but I leapt at the chance.

The interview was perfunctory. A trip to El Camino Drive to join a long line of hopefuls. I got looked at up and down and was hired with a commandment to stop shaving, which I was only doing twice a week. I was thrilled to be an extra, but the job soon turned into something more.

Extras spend most of the time off camera waiting around to mill around briefly on camera. One day, I was waiting in my Roman peasant outfit for the next crowd scene, when an assistant director motioned me over, handed me five dollars, and told me to find him a corned beef sandwich on light rye with plenty of mustard. He turned away, too busy to suggest where I could find such a thing. I ran out of the studio, up and down Radford Avenue, and found a deli just a block and a half away.

"Put extra mustard on that," I said.

The assistant director was so pleased, he appointed me what he called special assistant to the assistant. "Right, sure," I said. He said no, he wasn't kidding and looked at me with some interest. When he asked, "What's your name, kid?" I seized my chance.

My favorite things to watch on Aunt May's little TV were old B Westerns, and one of my heroes was Ray "Crash" Corrigan. I told my new boss my name was Bruce Corrigan. "Okay, Bruce," he said and handed me a sheaf of papers, told me to deliver them to the second assistant cinematographer. What a day! Not only was I now more than an extra, but I wasn't Harvey Stump.

I didn't tell Aunt May about changing my name. Though I was over the moon at the same time I felt guilty, as if I'd spit on my dead parents. And I wasn't sure I was free of Stump or ever would be. It ate at me.

The movie we were working on was *Spartacus* and Bryno Productions was owned by its star, Kirk Douglas. My boss, the assistant director, was a nice guy but always looked harassed and anxious as though he was afraid of getting fired. The film was in trouble. It was way over budget and taking forever. Douglas and the new director, Stanley Kubrick, were at each other's throats. The complications of the thing were staggering. 187 stuntmen had to be trained as gladiators. 7,000 tons of armor had to be borrowed from Italian museums and delivered to a location in Spain. Dalton Trumbo, the chief scriptwriter, was still on the blacklist; and there was grumbling that the movie was Communist propaganda. Some of the actors were doing vanity rewrites of their own scenes and argued with Douglas about them. Nothing was completed on schedule. There's a story about Peter Ustinov. His daughter was born the week shooting started. When she got to kindergarten, her teacher asked what her father did, and the little girl answered "Spartacus".

Being called Bruce wasn't easy to get used to, and I still didn't feel right about it. One afternoon after we'd shut down for the day, my boss asked why I always hesitated when he called me, and I confessed.

"Because it's not my real name," I said feeling worse than a phony, a sinner. "I'm sorry."

He guffawed. "But this is Hollywood!" he said. "Think my real name's Mitchell Breckinridge? Nope, Moses Blumenthal. I changed it when I came out here, when I still hoped I'd be in front of the camera instead of behind it."

"What?"

He began ticking off the famous names I'd been hearing for weeks.

"Kirk Douglas? Issur Danielovich. Tony Curtis? Bernie Schwartz. John Garfield? Julius Garfinkle. John Hoyt? John Hoystadt. John Gavin? John Golenor. Remember that first director who got fired, Anthony Mann? Emil Bundesmann. But my absolute favorite has got to be Herbert Lom. The Herbert's legit but not the Lom. Wait. I had to write that one down; it's a whopper." He reached for his wallet, removed a small piece of paper, unfolded it, and read it out slowly. "Herbert Charles Angelo Kuchacevich ze Schluderpacheru. How about *that*!"

"You mean *every*body here changed their names?"

"Not *every*body. Jean Simmons is really Jean Simmons—at least so far as I know. But it's Hollywood. Look, Bruce, it's California. Maybe it's America. It's stacked against Stump and Golenor, even *by* the Stumps and Golenors, but it'll throw its arms around a Douglas or a Garfield. Start over. Light out. Toss the past on the dustheap. History is bunk. America reads like Hebrew, from right to left. Change your name, change your fate. Act even when you're not."

I stared at him.

"Say, how'd you come up with Bruce Corrigan?"

I told him about my fondness for Crash Corrigan's Westerns, that I thought the name was cool.

He smiled at my evaporating innocence and misgivings; it was a kindly, indulgent sort of smile.

"You mean?"

"Raymond Benitz."

3. *Les Chiffres Sont des Prix, Les Noms Sont des Histoires - Marche Nuptiale Vexée en Mi Bémol Mineur pour Instruments à Vent Féminins*

George Hardy Dandridge asked me to marry him during Spring Break of my last year at Wellesley. He did it as he did most things, traditionally and with class. We were paying our second visit to his family, staying at their big mansion in Fairfax, Virginia, ostensibly in separate rooms. Spring comes early in Virginia. The magnolias and dogwoods were already in bloom, and it had been a long cold winter in Massachusetts One gorgeous morning, George, who had endured the same gray, frigid Yankee weather I had while finishing up his thesis at MIT, announced he was taking me to Providence Park for a picnic.

He lugged the big wicker basket from the station wagon, and I carried a plaid blanket. As I recall, his mother had packed the basket with real Virginia ham sandwiches on home-made sourdough, early peaches, half a chocolate cake, one thermos full of cold cucumber soup and another with sweet tea. The weather was so fine that we decided against picnicking in the pavilion and chose a place on the grass, in the sun. Because we were seated on the blanket, George had to get up, not down, on his knees, and fish in his pocket for the ring. He held it out in one hand but, before I could say anything, before I could throw my arms around him, he held up his other hand. "Not yet," he said grinning. As if fulfilling a rehearsed protocol, he said, "Your father gave me his permission when we visited at Christmas." Only then, as they say, did he pop the question. Apparently, marriage proposals, like bottles of champagne, have to be popped. Anyway, George got the answer we'd agreed on long before. His solemnity about the whole thing made me want to giggle but I managed to stifle it. As we hugged, I wondered if my father might have felt the same hilarity when asked for his formal blessing.

Wellesley and MIT had a sort of entente cordiale. George and I met at a mixer during my sophomore year. We danced and we dated, we dated some more, slept together, ate with friends at Cambridge restaurants, skied in Vermont, had a Valentine's weekend on Cape Cod. We sweated but survived the state visits to our parents: separate bedrooms in Fairfax but not in Larchmont. We'd be graduating the same week. It was all so tidy.

George was even-tempered and forbearing. I only made him angry once that I can remember. This was on our first visit to Virginia and that big handsome house with the all-round porch. "It's rather grand," I observed. "Do Episcopalian priests make that much?" George's father was a man of the cloth. He explained that the Dandridges had been in Virginia a long time. There was family money. "So," I said snippily "tobacco and slavery?" That was what made him mad. He'd never mentioned that he was from Southern aristocracy, so it wasn't my fault. He was proud of his family but maybe a little ashamed of it, too. Perhaps it was sticking my finger in that little sore that angered him. Later, when we both tried to laugh it off, he told me that the Hart in the middle of his name was his mother's maiden name. He added that the mother of Douglas MacArthur was a Hart, a relative. I couldn't be sure if he was proud of it or not.

This was in the mid-seventies, a heady time at Wellesley, especially in the dorms. There was so much to digest, decide about, debate, to be thrilled by. The Pill. Title Nine. Roe versus Wade. Consciousness-raising. Bra-burning. The ERA. Betty Friedan. Gloria Steinem. Kate Chopin. Gwendolyn Brooks. Adrienne Rich. Susan Brownmiller. Kate Millet. Inclusive Sisterhood displaced exclusive Sorority; Flight Attendants were in Stewardesses out. Liberation permeated the air of Severance Hall like patchouli, like tear gas at demonstrations. We privileged college girls were certain we needed liberating and we knew from what. We knew from our reading, the news, each other. We knew it from dissecting our boyfriends, fathers, brothers, and uncles. We knew from our mothers, too—from their examples, not from their lips. The poet Lynn Sukenick had just invented a word for the apprehension we were feeling, matrophobia.

By senior year, the bandwagon had grown loud, crowded, and exhilaratingly militant. I was half on it, half not. The half that wasn't on board belonged to the handsome, courtly, adoring, and dependable George Hart Dandridge.

I was not the only Wellesley senior to get engaged that spring, but I was the only one in my circle— "our coven," as Julia called us. The prospect of bridesmaids' dresses and intoxicated groomsmen failed to enthrall my friends. They expressed their disapproval interrogatively. It ran from the passive aggressive ("What about your career?") to the actively hostile ("So, babies and Valium?"). They'd all vetted George and he'd passed muster; but that before he gave me the ring. Hannah, our radical lesbian, called it "the shackle".

"Are you going to take his name?" This simple, practical question turned into an objective correlative, even more than the diamond ring.

My options: keep my own name, become another Mrs. Dandridge, or, like an English aristocrat or half-assed feminist, hyphenate. Each alternative felt like a galleon wallowing with an overload of significance. I became obsessively indecisive. Foolishly, I shared my dilemma with George, who was flabbergasted. "What? You're not into that feminist fad, are you?" Worse yet, he shared it with his parents and a week later told me what they thought. It sounded like holding on to my name was a deal-breaker for the Old Dominion.

Fury turned me childish. I wanted Mommy.

That Saturday, I took an early train to New York and a damn-the-expense cab all the way out to Larchmont.

My mother and I sat in the kitchen. She'd sent my father out on an errand. She sipped tea and I didn't.

"Well, dear, you know what *I* did. But times change. I'm proud of what you young women are doing. I can see your problem—good and bad on every side. But what do you really want?"

"That's just it. I don't know."

She looked at me and smiled sympathetically, maybe a bit ruefully. "Really?"

"What do you mean?"

She sighed and sipped. "If you love George, is it such a bad thing to take his name? Yes, I get that it's not exactly fashionable at Wellesley. I agree the custom's—what's the word?—patriarchal; but, well, that's how family names are made, including ours. Your father's job at the wedding is to give you away."

"But… I don't want to be *given away.* I'm not some old cat looking for a new owner."

"You say you're not sure about the name. Are things all right between you and George?"

"What? Yes. What do you mean?"

"Are you sure about George?"

"Do I love him?"

"I'm asking what your gut tells you, not your heart."

"My gut?"

She pointed at her abdomen.

Realizing and confessing at the same time, I said, "It tells me not to change my name."

Mother didn't give me any approval and she didn't criticize. She just made a noise and suggested I have a talk with my father when he got back with the half-dozen ears of fresh corn.

My father taught at Columbia and wrote esoteric articles about early American history, but his books were biographies. He'd written three about the Transcendentalists, Emerson, Thoreau, and the Alcotts. Then, around the time I went off to college, he'd switched to something different, the theater. He wrote a biography of Eugene O'Neill that won a prize. It paid for the new leather couch in the living room which I sat on as I laid out the problem for my father after he got back from the corn-run.

"It's not just the name business. It's the whole thing. I haven't really done anything yet. I'm afraid that marriage is going to close everything down. That's what my friends all think. I don't want to make a mistake." I didn't say, "like mother."

At first, he seemed just to duck the matter at hand, as if he was too wrapped up in his own concerns to focus on mine.

"I'm working on a new biography," he said.

"But Daddy—"

"It's about the first American woman to be a professional playwright. Ever hear of Martha Morton?"

"No," I said nearly exasperated.

My father hardly ever gave me a straight answer. Whenever I asked him the meaning of some obscure new word I'd come across in my reading, he'd point to the big dictionary on top of the bookcase. "Look it up." I suppose he thought it would make me think more or deeper or for myself. A lot of professors like being indirect.

"Martha Morton wrote this play called *A Bachelor's Romance*. The critics panned it, but it made her $250,000. And that was around the turn of the century, so real money, a fortune. She was famous. She was directing on Broadway at twenty-one. In 1904, she started an interview by saying 'Womanhood is a tragedy today. My next play will be about suffrage for women.'"

I was catching on. "So, she was a feminist ahead of her time?"

"A feminist for sure but very much *of* her time. She was doing well on her own, a model and mentor to others, a glowing example of the kind of woman she put into all her plays—an independent woman. Nevertheless, she married at thirty-two."

"Why?"

My father shrugged. "Fell in love? Wanted to give wedlock a try? Maybe for security? Anyway, she married a man named Hermann Conheim, a Jewish businessman."

"Was that daring?"

"She probably thought so."

I hesitated and realized my father was waiting for me to ask. "Did she change her name?"

"Nope. She made a million dollars; she founded the Society of Dramatic Authors, and she said women should take a role in solving the problems of society."

"Good for Martha."

"Well, yes. On the other hand, she never expressed much interest in those problems. She lived in New York City when immigration was at its height, when the filthy tenements were crammed and toddlers were dying in droves, when the only work for women was in sweatshops. She took no interest in the thriving Yiddish theater and had nothing to do with immigrant feminists or labor organizers. No Jews appear in her plays. And, so far as I can tell, she never mentioned her husband in public."

It was working. He was making me think. "So, Martha Morton didn't change her name and her husband didn't mind?"

"I have no idea what Hermann Conheim thought. I expect he was proud of his Gentile wife. But who knows what he really felt. Maybe they argued about it. Maybe she pointed out that her bad play had made a quarter of a million dollars."

"So, what are you telling me?"

My father was fond of this obscure book that ended with a long list of proverbs which he made me read. He liked quoting them. "Remember Verheim's proverbs?"

"Sure."

"I'm thinking of one."

"Which?"

He raised an arm and smiled. "All numbers are prices; all names are stories."

It was on the train back to Boston that I made up my mind.

Franklin W. Dixon

1. A Brief History

"As oil had its Rockefeller, literature had its Stratemeyer," wrote *Fortune* magazine of Edward Stratemeyer (1860-1930), a New Jersey high-school graduate of entrepreneurial genius. He began writing to kill time while working in the family tobacco shop, where his brother was his boss. Stratemeyer produced about thirteen hundred books, but what he's known for is inventing the boys and girls series, the Rover Boys, Hardy Boys, Dana Girls, the Bobbsey Twins, Tom Swift, and Nancy Drew. He made careful note of what sold and stuck with the formula. He was clever about marketing strategies, like making the kids' books look like adult ones. He organized industrial-style mass literary production. Not for nothing did his first employee, Charles Leslie McFarlane, dub him "the Henry Ford of fiction." But unlike Ford and Rockefeller, Stratemeyer kept his name out of the public eye. Instead of becoming a celebrity, he became a syndicate. A syndicate doesn't have a mustache and isn't driven by sibling rivalry, just simple greed for staggering sales. If it had a soul, the Stratemeyer Syndicate would have that of an insatiable slave driver.

Stratemeyer hired generations of hacks. Unknown themselves, they wrote under pseudonyms known to millions of children. Kids pictured these authors' handsome, comely faces, imagined their happy, fulfilled lives. The pseudonyms weren't pen-names, which are for individuals. What Stratemeyer pioneered was the *house* name. The Nancy Drews were written by Carolyn Keene, The Bobbsey Twins by Laura Lee Hope, Tom Swifts by Victor Appleton. House names were always WASP names, the kind agents used to pin on ethnic actors. The best known of Stratemeyer's house names is that of the author of the interminable Hardy Boys series, Franklin W. Dixon.

Stratemeyer's books were deplored by many, including the head of the Boy Scouts. The Newark Public Library banned them in 1901. Stratemeyer's response to that was famous among the staff for being like all his memoranda: succinct, smug, profit-minded, and to the point: "Taking them out of the Library has more than tripled sales in Newark."

2. Working Conditions

We'd all read Stratemeyer products when we were kids, enough to say we despised them. Trash, we all agreed, especially those of us who'd devoured them before hitting puberty.

We were all men, all young, all badly paid. We'd been recruited in one of three ways. The Syndicate cleverly placed ads in the kind of literary magazines in which we'd hoped to be published but weren't. They maintained contacts with literary agents who turned down our autobiographical first novels but said they knew of a place that might pay us to write. At a grim party or dingy watering hole, we'd run into somebody already working for Stratemeyer—or, just as often, who'd just quit. "It's awful, but you could give it a shot." Successful writers didn't become Franklin W. Dixon.

The factory was a big open space too brightly lit and flimsily divided into cubicles, each with a desk, typewriter, and wastebasket. We had to produce three thousand words a day. After the editors got at them, they'd usually turn into less than a thousand. There were house rules. No drinking on the job, of course. No sentences over twenty words or words over three syllables; no metaphors; a minimum of adverbs; approximations of foreign accents permitted only for villains but never a foreign word; no mention of violent death, drugs, hunger, or sex of any variety; disrespect to parents, police, or politicians verboten; every chapter but the last to end in a suspenseful situation; every book to be of a standard length. The leading characters must never age, marry, or mature. If they learned anything in one book, it should be forgotten by the next one. Intellectually as well as physically, Stratemeyer characters are perpetual virgins.

In the bullpen there was both competition and camaraderie. As with all hierarchical organizations, the social lubricant was grievance and the foremost topic complaint. We were all trying to write our second novels or stories for *The New Yorker.* Everybody wanted out, but we all needed the money, paltry though it was.

"I tried to give the boys a Negro friend. I was going to call him Jack Johnson."

"Slashed?"

"In a breath."

"Get bawled out, did you?"

"You bet. What did *you* do wrong today?"

"I used the word *mysteriously*."

"Don't tell me. Two syllables too many."

"*And* an adverb!"

"How's your new book coming along?"

"Who has the time? Besides, I'm exhausted."

"I know. The other night, I was trying to work on this story idea and discovered that I've forgotten how to write."

"Try reading some poetry."

"Really?"

"They're mostly short and they clear the palate. I took a dose of Keats last night."

"Did it help?"

"Not really."

"Say, you haven't got a spare sawbuck by any chance?"

"You're kidding, right?"

"Christ, I hate it."

"What?"

"All this. Short sentences. Short words. Short readers."

"I hate Frank. Likewise Joe. And I can't bear their fucking father. Who came up with the name *Fenton* anyway?"

"Franklin W. Dixon."

"I hate Franklin W. Dixon, too."

3. The Pact

Friday was payday. A bunch of us would usually repair to McCallahan's, pony up for a single pitcher of beer, then whine at our ease and at length.

One Friday, somebody asked the table a question.

"What do you think the W's for?"

"The W?"

"You know. In Franklin W. Dixon."

The suggestions poured in.

"Wretched?"

"Wrong?"

"Got to be Wellington."

"Nah. Wages."

We laughed, then somebody made an almost serious suggestion.

"It stands for we—as in we're all Dixon."

"Shit, you're right. We *are* all Franklin W. Dixon."

"For our sins."

We grumbled a bit, then someone said, "Say, I've just had an idea."

"Hurt much?"

"What is it?"

"Wicked."

"Shoot, then."

There were eight of us around the table, nursing our tepid beer.

"Okay. We write our *own* Stratemeyers."

"Huh?"

"Four books. We work in pairs. A Nancy Drew, a Tom Swift, a Bobbsey Twins, and, of course, a Hardy Boys. What do you say?"

"What would we do with them?"

"Get a little of our own back."

"I see. Therapy."

"Stratepsychotherapy."

"What the hell. I'll give it a shot."

"Me, too. Why not? Can't write anything decent anyway."

We gave ourselves a deadline, a generous, non-Stratemeyer one of three months.

It turned out to be good fun of the adolescent kind, not wage-slavery but freely-chosen, vengeful labor.

Aram Ardekian and Joe Ricci drew the Bobbsey Twins but expanded on it and produced *The Bobbsey Twins and the Rover Boys in the Blitz*. The four plucky kids, moved by Edward R. Murrow's radio broadcasts, stow away on a freighter. Their plan is to make their way to London where they'll help all the Mr. and Mrs. Minnivers. They take the long train ride from Liverpool to Euston Station where they see lines of brave little children lined up to leave the city, stoic fathers and crying mums beside them. The air smells of burning and night is falling. Undaunted, the four go looking for lodgings. They happen to be in Aldemanbury Square when Brewers' Hall takes a direct hit and collapses on them.

Hugo Gerstner and Billy Mulligan wrote *Tom Swift Builds A Jet Plane*. It was predictable. Tom constructs the plane with the help of a crusty but kind old engineer who, for some reason, can't stop touching him. When the plane's finished, Tom takes it up for a solo test flight. The engine flames out and the plane crashes right into his father's business, the biggest one in Shopton, the Swift Construction Company. The crusty engineer survives but not Tom's father. Shopton becomes a derelict town full of unemployed men, drunks, and drug addicts. All the high school cheerleaders become streetwalkers.

"Swift Deconstruction," somebody cracked after we'd shared our work.

Stash Wojciechowski and Alex Cendenjas pushed things pretty far with *Nancy Drew and the Creep Next Door*, a tale in which the busybody heroine, investigating her new neighbor, is molested by him. Traumatized to the point of aphasia and catatonia, she's committed to an asylum for the rest of her life.

I still have the typescript of the book I wrote with Harvey Finkelstein. We called it *The Hardy Boys and the Mass Murderer* because the term serial killer hadn't yet been coined. Bayport is terrorized by a series of brutal killings characterized by inventive mutilations. Frank and Joe spring into action. Their suspicions fall on the town's only Jew, Mordechai Mendelssohn, proprietor of a shop locally known as "the Jew store," the only one open on Sundays. The boys notice that the murders all happen on Saturday nights. They spy on Mendelssohn and track him. One Saturday night, the boys follow him to the edge of town and see him slip into the abandoned barn on the old Cabot place. Cautiously, they open the creaking door and are immediately felled by two blows delivered with a maul. They are then expertly castrated, dismembered, and buried in the pleasant little wood behind Bayport High.

Harvey and I soon left Stratemeyer for other jobs. I turned into an academic; Harvey went on to a lucrative career writing B-movie scripts in Hollywood. We kept in touch for a few years. In one of his last letters, Harvey credited his success to his apprenticeship with the Syndicate. "Stratemeyer taught me how to collaborate with cynics, follow idiotic rules, and crank out crap against a deadline. I owe him everything."

I still remember the flourish with which Harvey extracted his fountain pen from his jacket, unscrewed the top, and ceremoniously signed the title page of our puerile parody and protest. It's right here on my yellowed copy in Harvey's big Hancock-like letters: Franklin W. Dixon.

Akewi

1. My Life Before

My name was Fritz and I disliked it as much as the man who pinned it on me. A dark-haired, conceited, flabby Johannes was an exchange student far more interested in women than books. So far as I could tell, he had respect for neither. The difference was that he perpetually sought out the former and avoided the latter. Apart from romantic pursuits, his favorite pastimes were drinking alcohol, eating take-out food, listening to techno music, and looking at pornography.

What would such a person want with me? It certainly was a question. I thought about it and concluded that he installed me in his disorderly flat to impress the women he managed to lure there. The idea must have been to make them think he had a soft side, that he was capable of sincere affection. I gathered that these women thought him exotic; they liked his accent. They all approached my cage with the identical silly smile and asked my name. "Oh," Johannes would say with a grin, "that's my faithful comrade, Fritz." "He looks sad," some would say. "Do you ever let him out so he can fly around?" One said, "He has such intelligent eyes." All of them asked if I could talk. "When he likes," Johannes would reply coyly. "He's got a mind of his own, does Fritz; but he's a dear, good boy." This pretense of devotion really did make a good impression on the women, at least at first. In fact, Johannes fed me irregularly, often neglected to clean out my cage and to keep the water fresh. When the women wanted to how he came to own me, he told the same story about saving me from a filthy bazaar during the year he spent in Africa doing humanitarian work. To forestall premature departures by the women, Johannes taught me a speech. When one of them headed for the door, he would clap his hands and I was to say, "*Wie geht es dir, Fräulein? Geh nicht. Ich liebe dich.*"

It worked surprisingly well. The woman would stop and ask Johannes to translate. This he did in a manner he probably thought irresistibly charming. It took me a long time to learn that little speech, and Johannes was hardly a patient teacher. He yelled at me and slapped my cage when I got a word wrong or if my pronunciation was faulty. At the time, I had no idea what the words meant, though I did understand they had to mean something—something that could make a woman who wanted to get away from Johannes reconsider doing so.

I too longed to get away from Johannes but had no idea how to go about it. I couldn't simply fly away, not with my clipped wings. Besides, Johannes never opened my cage except to change the newspaper that lined its bottom. Even then, he kept me from hopping out with a long fork. Eventually, I decided my only recourse was to find some way to make him wish to be rid of me. But, even if I could find that way, the risk was terrifying. He might have left me to die of thirst or simply twisted my neck. He was capable of either. If I irritated him when he was in a fury—for instance, just after a woman had walked out—he might just toss me out the window. My first and last flight.

I bided my time.

Something changed. Johannes was bringing back only one woman. She stayed over nights and then entire weekends. Her name was Juliet, and I could see how it was. Johannes went from being kind and loving toward Juliet to sounding sarcastic and angry. Twice I saw him grab her arm while he shouted at her. I paid close attention. Then one night the two of them returned and Johannes was already yelling at Juliet. As usual, he'd been drinking and he went on drinking after they came in, growing more furious with each gulp. Juliet expostulated with him, apparently denying something. And then suddenly, if I understood correctly, she too became angry and stopped denying anything. Johannes exploded. He threw his beer can in her direction and ran to the door, violently yanking it open.

"Get out!" he shouted. *"Raus mit dir! Raus mit dir, du. . . du Schlampe*!"

Raus mit dir, du Schlampe. I let these words sink in; I could tell they were powerful. I memorized them and waited to unleash them. Last year, when I was being read an old play, a couple lines reminded me of the feeling I often had during my time with Johannes: *I understand a fury in your words but not your words.* When I think back to that unhappy epoch, I can appreciate and even identify with Desdemona's double innocence. Unlike Johannes' cheating girlfriend, Desdemona had not betrayed Othello; but she was also innocent in being unable to make out the sense of an angry speech. That's just how I was back then, hearing noises, knowing they signified something, but unable to make out what.

I did escape, of course. I'd like to think that my cleverness and bravery were rewarded, but the truth is that I was just spectacularly lucky.

Juliet never returned, and it was a long time before Johannes brought a new woman back to the apartment. The two of them came in tipsily and fell together on the couch. I waited until they were entangled before delivering my speech as loudly as I could: *Raus mit dir, du Schlampe!*

Everything stopped. Johannes leapt up. The woman, alarmed, cried, "What was that? What did he say?"

Johannes tried to calm her.

I said it again. *Raus mit dir!* And said it again and again. . . until she left. Johannes was beside himself.

I played this scene three times with three different women.

Johannes made threats; he roared and shook his fist. Once, he whacked my cage so violently that I fell off my perch and hurt my head. But this only encouraged me.

I began to say the phrase at random times, even when he was asleep. *Raus mit dir!*

I don't doubt that Johannes would have liked to kill me. But he also wanted money and he had bought me from a pet shop. This meant I had value, and so, instead of wringing my neck and stuffing me into a garbage bag, he sold me. I've never asked for how much and I've never been told. But I do know that he posted flyers on bulletin boards around the university. One of these was spotted by my savior, Leda, the love of my life. She bought me, redeemed me. It is Leda who has made me the focus of her life and work, as she is of mine. It is Leda who gave me a new life, a purpose, and immensely more. It is Leda who changed the despicable Fritz to the noble Akewi.

2. Leda

The first thing I want to stress about Leda is that she is kind. When she came to take me away from Johannes she whispered to me soothingly, as though reassuring me that our bond would be nothing like the one from which she was rescuing me. Of course, she couldn't know my feelings about Johannes. She was only anxious that I would be upset about being moved. How could she have known how delighted and relieved I was? I remember trying to indicate this to her by hopping up and down and mimicking her whisper.

The second thing to say about Leda is that she's a scientist. This means she saw me as a research subject, though our relationship soon became something closer and more intimate, a collaboration. Our work reinforced our attachment like a pair of oxen yoked to the same load, pulling it up the same hill. My progress was hers.

As a teenager, Leda had read about Alex and Irene Pepperberg and was moved by their story. Learning about them set the course of her life—therefore of mine. Like Leda, Dr. Pepperberg had given a significant name to her subject and friend. "Alex" was an acronym for

Avian Language Experiment. The two worked together for three decades. It was slow going but both persisted. At the time of his death, Alex had a vocabulary of a hundred words. He could ask and answer questions, distinguish colors and shapes. He grasped spatial relations: above, below, over, under. He was able to make requests, such as asking to stop working when he was tired. Notably, Alex was able to teach behaviors to other birds, becoming, in a sense, a lab assistant. Dr. Pepperberg estimated that Alex had the intelligence of a five-year-old child, certainly on a par with dolphins and apes. The scientific world was more than skeptical. Birds have bird brains, they said, and they aren't mammals. But the evidence was undeniable.

What caught Leda's imagination was that Dr. Pepperberg, though she never claimed two-way communication, said that, when he died at thirty-one, Alex had not achieved his full potential. Creatures like Alex and me can live forty-five years or more.

Leda told me the sad story of how, when Dr. Pepperberg came to the lab one morning, she found Alex dead. She spoke movingly of the dreadful shock Dr. Pepperberg must have suffered and the mourning that followed. I was touched too and understood that Leda was imagining how she would feel if I were to die. She told me that Alex's last words were the ones he spoke to Dr. Pepperberg every night when she left the lab: *You look good. See you tomorrow. I love you.* As she told me this, Leda wept. I had never seen her cry before. I wanted to comfort her.

When Leda leaves me for the night, I sometimes think of both Alex and Johannes and say, *Geh nicht. Ich liebe dich.* It's a serious but private joke.

Item three: Leda is patient and unfailingly encouraging. She rejoices in any progress I achieve, ascribing it all to me when it is more her doing than mine.

Item the fourth: Leda is beautiful.

3. Breakthroughs

The speech that liberated me from Johannes taught me that words could provoke feelings. But, at the time, I couldn't grasp all the implications; I didn't yet think of words as words but merely as sounds. The difference is vital. If Alex had figured out the connection between sound and significance, then it's not surprising Dr. Pepperberg thought he might have achieved more. If one Congo Grey could go where all the experts thought impossible why shouldn't another go still further? This was the goal of Leda's research project. It became mine as well.

I liked my new home in the laboratory. It made a change from Johannes' untidy and dingy flat and my filthy old cage. Everything was clean and white, and my cage was far larger than the old one and scrupulously maintained. Better still, I was allowed out of it for hours at a time. Leda even made a special perch for me by her desk. The dowel wasn't too thin or thick but just right. And there was a high window I could look out whenever I liked. During the day I could see sunlight, clouds, and trees. At night, there was the big moon and the countless little stars.

At first, our work was just a kind of playing with sounds. My earliest efforts were senseless noises, then equally meaningless rhymes. These rhymes pleased me because they delighted Leda. Whenever I made one, she would give me a special treat, a bit of melon, mango, a strawberry—or pieces of carrot, sweet potato. With such encouragement I croaked out plenty of nonsense.

What sight like
Purple strike

Brown pinch
Salt on inch
Bright light
Cage tight

Then, one afternoon—I've never figured out quite how—I managed to fit rhyme to reward:

Want treat
Something sweet

When Leda heard that, she did a jig around the lab. Watching her dance was even better than the strawberry I earned.

For a time, Leda took on an assistant. Selena wasn't much interested in me. She favored the white mice who never said anything, at least nothing either she or I could hear. Her duties were to take notes on experiments and to keep the lab clean. She asked Leda endless questions about how to get ahead in animal psychology. When she was alone cleaning up, she liked to listen to music, but I couldn't hear it because she had these wires that kept it in in her ears. I didn't even know she was listening to music until the time the wires fell out and I heard the faint beat.

One day, Selena brought a box that put out plenty of sound. It was music but also words. I was afraid Selena might turn it off, so I hopped up and down, bobbed my head, and squawked: "Good good mood. Good like food."

One song attracted me powerfully. I beat my wings against the cage so Selena would play it again and, to my delight, she did. It amused her that I liked this song. She came over to my cage and laughed at me. That was an important day.

Years later, I found out the song was called "Around the Way Girl." It's long and most of it passed right through me; but one line stuck. Like Desdemona, I understood the passion in the words, just not the words. Somehow—maybe because of my infatuation with Leda—I intuited that it was a love song, even though the singer didn't sound loving.

Silky milky, her smile is like sunshine

I tried to memorize these words the way I had the ones Johannes taught me. I practiced over and over and, two mornings later, when Leda came into the lab, I greeted her with *Silky milky, her smile is like sunshine.*

Leda thought the words were mine until she told Selena about it. Selena laughed and explained they were LL Cool J's. All the same, Leda was wowed. That was the day she began to call me Akewi. In Africa, it means poet.

Leda began reading to me. She started with nursery rhymes—*Jack and Jill went up the hill. . . Georgie Porgy puddin' and pie. . . .* Then she moved on to short but more challenging poems—*Never met this fellow attended or alone / without a tighter breathing and zero at the bone. . . Loveliest of trees, the cherry now / is hung with bloom along the bough. . . .* Whenever I liked a particular bit, I'd try to repeat it.

Gradually, Leda expanded the scope of our readings; but, for a long time, she chose only rhyming poems. I was often bored or exasperated by understanding so little and I let her see it by closing my eyes or reeling on my perch as if I were about to fall off. But Leda persisted. It was as though she wanted to drown me in verse. Little by little, my vocabulary grew, and I began to understand more with less strain. Nevertheless, I never found the relation between sound and meaning easy to grasp.

For a long time, Leda read out of the same book. This was a fat little paperback called *Immortal Poems of the English Language.* It featured portraits of the poets on the front and back covers. Whenever she was going to read me something by one of them, Leda showed me the portrait first. I liked that. They were all so different from one another. I wanted to meet them. Leda explained why this was impossible. That was a shocking lesson.

The most lasting impressions were made by a poem by Dylan Thomas and another by Percy Shelley. It was hearing these poems over and over that did the most for my ability to connect sound to sense.

"Poem in October" thrilled me. It wasn't clear but didn't need to be as it was as much music as words and the music was intoxicating.

. . .Here fond climates and sweet singer suddenly
Come in the morning when I wandered and listened
To the rain wringing
Wind blow cold
In the wood faraway under me.

Years later, when Leda told me about Alex, dead at thirty-one, I thought of this poem's first line: *It was my thirtieth year to heaven.* By then I was myself well over thirty.

I couldn't take in all of what Dylan Thomas wrote, of course, even though I made Leda read his words again and again.

Fond climates was puzzling but pleasing to repeat. And I liked the way *The wood faraway under me* shifted things, as if the poem shot up to take a bird's-eye view. The words seemed to awaken some atavistic impulse in me, perhaps a recovered memory of unclipped wings, though I've never flown above a wood, above anything.

When I finally figured out the distinction between *wringing* and *ringing,* I was proud but also baffled that two words could sound the same but mean different things. Like learning about the death of Alex, it was an unsettling revelation. I thought about it for a long time.

Shelley's poem spoke to me more directly than "Poem in October." I liked to think he had me in mind, Akewi, as he wrote it.

Hail to thee, blithe spirit!
Bird thou never wert;

That from Heaven, or near it,
Pourest thy full heart
In profuse strains of unpremeditated art. . .

. . . Like a poet hidden
In the light of thought
Singing hymns unbidden
Till the world is wrought
To sympathy with hope and fears it heeded not..

I loved the word skylark. Leda explained that it is a bird that sings beautifully and suggested that the poet identified himself with it. I liked the idea of Shelley comparing himself to the skylark and admitting he came in second:

Better than all measures
Of delightful sound
Better than all treasures
That in books are found
Thy skill to poet were, thou scorner of the ground!

Maybe Shelley wanted to be both a poet and a bird. I wanted to be a bird poet and a poet too, like the skylark and like Shelley. I too longed to *scorn the ground*, to soar. This poem felt like it was calling to me, and I determined I would do my best to merit the name Leda had given to me. Akewi. Poet.

4. Premeditated Unpremeditated Art

There was so much to learn. To begin with, I would need a decent vocabulary. Alex's hundred words would hardly serve and, though I had already exceeded that number, what I had was still pitiful.

Leda's belief is that language isn't acquired from lessons or dictionaries but from swimming in the sea of language, flying through a sky thick with floating words. She read something to me every day for ten minutes. When she saw how keen I was to learn, she set up a machine near my cage that played recordings of stories and plays but mostly poems. I had a switch that I could peck to turn the voices on and off. If I wanted, I could listen all night and often, too excited to sleep, I did just that. At other times, the voices droned, and I fell asleep in minutes. Over the years, my vocabulary and confidence swelled until I felt ready to make my first serious effort at composition. It was painstaking and exasperatingly slow; moreover, the result was crude and didn't make very good sense. Nevertheless, from Leda's response you'd think I'd produced an avian *Divine Comedy*.

Let those in, but stay outside;
close the cage, just not too wide.

Bestir yourself while you're at rest;
your worst is better than my best.

The stars are out, the sky's black blue;
the clock runs slowly, one to two.

One meal a day makes not a fast;
an unfed bird's not apt to last.

Endure the storm and pay your dues,
regret nothing, ignore the news.

Keep bad folk out after you go;
if they say yes, then we'll say no.

Leda transcribed it. She also gave it a title so she could file it properly. She called it "Akewi's Advice."

My second attempt was better, at least in my opinion. Leda makes no distinctions between good and bad. Whatever I produce thrills her, an enthusiastic audience but useless as a critic. On the other hand, she excels at inventing titles. This one she called "Gnomic Song":

Belly of a blue-scaled fish,
tigrous eye, unblinking, wide,
an ink-stained mirror on a dish,
to show those things that shadows hide.

Arcanae in roots of heather,
chthonous rumbling under clods:
if gods didn't make the weather,
surely weather made the gods.

Rivers wrap a smooth white stone,
storms blow soft through hollow reeds,
interpenetrating bone,
blood and marrow, wings and seeds.

Go pluck pits from brittle pods,
a song from lungs fretted with feather.
If weather hasn't made the gods,
Surely gods have made the weather.

Where did I learn of the gods? From the *Odyssey* and a book of Greek myths. Leda was astonished by *chthonous* and *arcanae* but the word she liked best of all was *tigrous*, because I'd made it up.

We had been together for more than a decade by then. They were good years, filled with listening, learning, composing. I consumed far more than I produced. Leda finished her thesis, and it was published, an impressively thick book with a blue cover, a real book like *Immortal*

Poems of the English Language. So, I was an author, too. Though most of it was Leda's writing, her data and charts, it included my verses as well, all neatly printed. "Look," she said, and showed me the cover. It was a picture of Leda and me. "We're famous, Akewi."

She was right. Soon there came reporters and photographers, interviewers, then airplanes, audiences, applause. From adults there was skepticism and condescension, from children curiosity and awe. For our public appearances, Leda wore make-up and colorful clothes. She cut her hair, too. I didn't care for all these changes but kept it to myself.

Did I have mixed feelings? Of course I did. Being famous made Leda happy but it divided us and took us away from home. Worse still were those times I stayed in the lab while she flew off to one of her conferences to defend our work. That's when I learned what pining means, that you could resent what you yearned for. Out of that soup of feelings I spooned these verses:

Cage's dents make ragged shade,
and newsprint is no gladsome guide:
away from bright cold steel tables
all's deranged, detached, denied.

How am I doing? what
poignantly remember?
Perhaps I'll tell next Monday,
or maybe in November.

From me to you to me
from you to me to you—
Akewi unfeathered, alone, forlorn,
like the last bird in the zoo.

5. My Fortieth Year to Heaven

Leda thinks I'm ten years older than Alex when he fell off his perch, a whole decade. I don't want to go gentle into that good night, Dylan Thomas, honestly, I don't. To rage is respectable. To rage is dignified. But is it admirable only because it's futile? Like Alex, you never made it to your fortieth birthday, Dylan Thomas, and by then you'd been raging for twenty years. You were just half my age when you wrote this:

When their bones are picked clean and the clean bones gone,
They shall have stars at elbow and foot.
And death shall have no dominion.
No more may gulls cry at their ears
Or waves break loud on the seashore.

Did you grasp it, being then so full of life, thinking there was so much of it ahead?

Leda is older too. Her hair is turning the color of my feathers. But to me her beauty has only deepened. The elastic enthusiasm of youth began to harden when she got her degree, but it has been replaced by a queenly seriousness. One thing has not changed at all; her devotion to me is undiminished. I see the anxiety in her face when she arrives each morning and the relief when she sees me doing my best to hop up and down at the sight of her.

During these last weeks I have been making a poem for Leda—a farewell poem, a valediction—but now that it's done, I can't bring myself to say it to her.

I took my theme and my title not from Dylan Thomas or Percy Shelley, not from any of the immortal poets of the English language, but from what an old philosopher said. John Keats, to my surprise, rated philosophy above poetry. *An eagle is not so fine a thing as a truth,* he explained. I'd like to argue that an eagle *is* a kind of truth; still, I know what he meant.

So Long as We Exist, Death is Not With Us

You in an airplane, I in a balloon.
The sky moves, and the clouds.
We move too. You fast and not low,
I far below and very slow.
You showed me us in a photograph.
It's a sort of proof, ocular proof,
you said, proof of our fame, you said.
The Congo Grey that loves you
will love you 'til he drops dead.

But When We Are Dead, Then We Do Not Exist

Silence isn't silent, sleep isn't sleeping,
darkness isn't dark, meaning isn't meaning.
The perch beneath me that I won't feel,
warm sunlight in our lab I will not feel.
Shall I drop down right now, shall I?
My cage will be spotless at last.
But I'll miss all the words I'll miss,
the songs, but most of all you.
Goodbye. Don't cry. Just blow a kiss.

No, I can't recite this to Leda. It's too much for me to bear. And, after all, there's no improving on what my more innocent precursor said.

You be good. See you tomorrow. I love you.
Ich liebe dich.

www.ingramcontent.com/pod-product-compliance
Lightning Source LLC
LaVergne TN
LVHW091048150826
845673LV00002B/510
9788119228355